Swan Sister

Do

Also by Annie Dalton

The Afterdark Princess
The Real Tilly Beany
Tilly Beany and the Best Friend Machine
The Witch Rose

for older readers

The Alpha Box
Naming the Dark
Night Maze
Out of the Ordinary

Swan Sister

Annie Dalton

MAMMOTH

*To Eve Norman, without whom I would never
have come to know and love East Suffolk,
to Miriam and Otis Hall, with gratitude,
and to Katie Macmillan who loves the wild swans.*

First published in Great Britain 1992
by Methuen Children's Books Ltd
Published 1993 by Mammoth
an imprint of Reed Consumer Books Ltd
Michelin House, 81 Fulham Road, London SW3 6RB
and Auckland, Melbourne, Singapore and Toronto

Copyright © 1993 Annie Dalton

The right of Annie Dalton to be identified as author of this
work has been asserted by her in accordance with the
Copyright, Designs and Patents Act 1988

ISBN 0 7497 1065 9

A CIP catalogue record for this title
is available from the British Library

Printed in Great Britain
by Cox & Wyman Ltd, Reading, Berkshire

Contents

1 The Dream House   1

2 The Broken Angel   10

3 Over the Edge of the World   23

4 Earth Child, Star Child   39

5 Enchanted   47

6 The Dark Tower   56

7 Feathers in the Wind   66

8 A Maze of Water   76

9 Swan Child   88

10 Midsummer's Eve   102

11 The Shining Ones   113

1

The Dream House

The scream of the American jets tore through the summer air, deafening Ellen and frightening a pair of swans into flight from their nesting place amongst the reeds. The swans took off for a short distance, then skidded down awkwardly like water-skiers in a flurry of dirty water, only inches from Ellen. She went on emptying sand out of her canvas shoe, bracing her hand on the scorching paintwork of the upturned boat as she balanced on one foot.

She was vaguely disappointed that, close up, these dingy birds were not snow white as she had always supposed. I don't like their eyes, she thought uneasily. Why are they looking at me like that? It's as if they can see right through me. As if I'm not really here at all.

Then the shadow slipped between Ellen and the sun. A shiver ran down her backbone as if someone had wrung out an ice-cold, soaking-wet cloth over her and the perfect summer's day flickered into a negative of itself. The dirty biscuit-coloured towers of the power station became a brooding, blackened castle overshadowing the little estuary town. The scream of the gulls was blotted out. A sudden wind sent dried seaweed skittering and a thin blade of a voice tried to hiss a warning.

Swa – swa siss swa siss.

'No,' said Ellen, desperately hopping, trying to get

her shoe back on. 'You're lying. Anyway I don't want to hear. Don't tell me.'

She had no idea what she was saying, only that in the split second of chill and darkness, a struggle of some kind was going on. And it seemed that Ellen won. At the moment she got her shoe back on the sun blazed again overhead.

Perhaps it's my new specs. They don't work properly, she thought.

Her goose-pimpled arms slowly returned to normal. The gulls carried on shrieking scandals. The two swans continued sailing up the oily waters of the estuary and Cass, Ellen's mother, still hummed as she sauntered along the street that led uphill from the quay.

She was taking a reel of film out of her camera while she waited for Ellen. She'd been snapping pictures of the houses they'd seen, to show Ellen's father when they got back to London. Cass had been in a wonderful mood ever since they'd arrived. Now, with her skirt of dull rose flapping against her long legs, her fair hair blowing across her face, she was the picture of contentment.

Yet for some reason, every time her mother said how happy she was that all the family's dreams were coming true at last, Ellen felt scared to death. She couldn't understand it. Until now she'd been famous in her family for being an easy-going child, needing little to keep her amused except a constant supply of books. And she was excited about the new baby, too, though she couldn't see how Cass could be so sure it was a girl.

But how could she tell her mother that, since their arrival, they'd been followed by a shadow, a shivering slice of shadow, and that a moment ago, as though the swans had opened an invisible doorway into her world, the shadow finally crept like a sorrowful ghost between Ellen and the sun; a ghost with a warning message.

And I don't want to hear, she thought wildly. Oh, I *don't* want to. And maybe it's just my glasses really. Maybe that's all it is.

Fastening her shoe with trembly hands, Ellen ran to catch her mother up, complaining at the top of her voice, needing to feel ordinary again, to break the shadow's power over her.

'I feel sandpapered all over,' she grumbled. She put her fingers gingerly to her cheek which felt sore from the rough tongue of the wind. 'My lips taste salty,' she added, surprised, squinting against the light.

'It's the healthiest place in the world,' said Cass, filling her lungs. 'When I lived here before I hardly had a cold. The sea breezes blew them away. Isn't it funny, Nell, you're the same age now as I was when I had to leave Suffolk. You're going to love it here so much.'

Ellen thought it was too soon to tell. After London, East Anglia seemed so clean, so bright. These cottages hurt her eyes with their dazzling ice-cream colours, their pebbly windblown gardens full of rose-pink hollyhocks and pale golden poppies. Wherever she looked she couldn't escape the glinting water, sunlight, shrieking white birds. A holiday was one thing. But *living* here so far from everything she knew. This was the shining edge of the world, Ellen thought. It would be too easy to fall over it and be lost forever.

But Ellen's mother had made up her mind. She had always longed to come back to the countryside where she'd lived until her parents died when she was seven. Through the years that followed Cass never forgot her dream of returning to Suffolk one day and giving her own children the happiness she remembered from those early years. Only this time there would be no tragic ending, and there'd be two children to be company for each other, whereas Cass had been a lonely only one. And now there was enough money to buy the kind of place she'd always dreamed of. Even Ellen's father agreed now that it was better to move out of London, especially since they were having a new baby at long last.

Ellen wished her father hadn't been too busy to come house-hunting. We should *all* be here, she thought. Her father had assured her that he didn't mind in the least.

'It's perfectly fair,' he'd said. He'd chosen their flat in London. He'd been living in it when Cass married him. 'Cass should choose our new home for our new country life. Anyway, I can't afford to take time off just now, Nell. It's a tricky time at work. And you honestly don't need me. I trust you both and Cass has perfect taste.'

But it felt unlucky to Ellen. Like walking under a ladder by mistake or forgetting to say 'rabbits' on the first of the month.

Besides, how could anyone be too busy to come and choose his own house?

'And how will he manage to get to his office?' she had worried as they drove down.

'Your father's always done some work from home,' Cass said happily. 'There are good trains to London. Or he can drive. A long country drive will help him unwind. And we're keeping the old flat so he can use it overnight if he needs to. You'll see, it'll be terribly simple.'

It sounded terribly complicated to Ellen.

She worried, too, what weird place her mum might buy, left to her own devices. Cass was a designer. So she mainly cared about how things looked, Ellen thought, or how interesting they seemed. If the house had a romantic tower or if some mad artist had once lived there, Cass would absolutely refuse to see the leaky drains or broken slates. She wouldn't care how uncomfortable it was. She'd get that gleam in her eye and that was that.

It was Ellen and her father who were the sensible ones. So why didn't he come with them to keep an eye on things, instead of telling Cass she could go ahead and buy her dream lighthouse or whatever it was she wanted to drag them all off to. 'Don't worry,' Ellen had heard him say to her mother. 'Whatever it is, I'll sign on the dotted line.' It was almost as if he didn't care what she did, Ellen thought.

Cass hadn't dragged Ellen off to a lighthouse yet but she'd been suspiciously enthusiastic about a falling-down mill and that disused railway station, Ellen thought, and the house-hunting trip wasn't over yet.

Ellen couldn't understand why it was supposed to be trendy to turn something into a home that was never intended to be one. Why couldn't the Carsons live in a house like other people, a normal, comfortable house like the kind her father designed for people?

'Do you fancy an ice cream while we're waiting for the last estate agent?' Cass asked. 'I need a rest. I'm sure I never got this tired when I was expecting you, Nell. But I suppose I'm an old lady now, to be having a baby and running around Suffolk on a wild-house chase.'

She laughed, patting her nearly flat stomach ruefully, but Ellen knew pretty Cass didn't really think thirty was old to have babies, and she wasn't really apologising for chasing so single-mindedly after dream houses either.

Cass believed Ellen was lucky to have such an

unusual woman for her mother. 'Most children have such a dull time,' she'd say. 'Stuck in front of videos all day. But you see life, Nell.'

'The estate agent said he'd meet us here,' Cass told her, as they perched on the wall outside a small private museum. Cass had suggested earlier that Ellen would like to look round it ('It always fascinated me when I was your age') but its dusty sunblistered window was full of incomprehensible maps with spidery writing on them, and through the doorway Ellen glimpsed dull cases full of broken pottery that made her yawn as soon as she set eyes on them, so she politely refused.

'Apparently we'd never find the place by ourselves,' Cass went on. 'So we've got to follow him down the lanes. And if there's time afterwards there's somewhere else I want to show you. It's a church, partly ruined, but quite a special one, with a very strange history. And all that's left of its graveyard is one single headstone, only inches from the cliff. All the rest fell over the edge hundreds of years ago.'

An alarming thought struck Ellen. A church, especially a ruined, dangerous one, with a romantic history sounded right up Cass's street.

'You don't want to live in it, do you?' she demanded. She could just imagine coming back from school to find the kitchen slithering over the cliff and Cass standing amongst their belongings, the baby in her arms, saying cheerfully, 'What do you think, Nell, isn't this a glorious view!'

'Heavens no.' Cass seemed surprised. 'But it's fairly close. A few minutes in the car. There's something I've always longed to show you, there. Something that was very special to me when I was a little girl. Would you like to see it?'

'I think so,' said Ellen doubtfully. 'Maybe.' After all,

she'd refused Cass's offering of the museum, she thought. Then she realised she'd bitten the end off her cornet by mistake and had to gobble the rest in a hurry to stop it splurging over her dress.

'It's quite safe,' said Cass laughing. 'I promise.' She began to cross her heart, when she stood up with a little shriek instead and began brushing down her skirt. She'd seen a glossy red car pulling up on the other side of the road.

'Here he is, I think,' she said. 'Our estate agent.'

'It isn't a lighthouse, is it?' Ellen asked with dread. 'The place he's taking us to see?'

'Not quite,' laughed Cass. 'Much as I'd love one.'

'Is this one just a house then, maybe?' asked Ellen, unable to disguise her longing.

'Not exactly,' said her mum. 'But I've got a good feeling about it. I think you'll like it. Honestly.'

As her mother carefully followed the estate agent's car through winding lanes into the dim tunnel of an ancient forest, Ellen felt the shadow's prickling return. She was suddenly too tired to fight it any more so this time there were no struggles, shocks, or shivers.

And instead of the day turning inside out and darkening, everything became at once both brilliantly clear and a long way off, as if she could see far too much of everything through a sparkling magic glass. Far too much.

Ellen snatched her glasses off, furiously blinking the vision away. But it was no use. This haunting had nothing to do with her specs.

Her mother's search was over. And it had been leading them here all the time.

They were not going to choose the house on the other side of this forest, Ellen realised, because the house had already chosen *them*. Cass's dream house

7

had been waiting for her a long time; secretly, magically calling to her, shaping her longings.

But why? And what was going to happen there?

Now Ellen was watching a second, reflected Ellen outside the car, gently floating amongst the leaves and branches of passing trees; she had Ellen's brown hair, her dark blue eyes with the sharp knowing expression she never meant to be there. As the car sped down the lanes lacy cow parsley, wild dog roses, even the scissoring shadows of birds flew eerily in and out of the reflection. This Ellen was not solid, or separate, but a girl of light and leaves, part of everything.

The house knew they were on their way at last. It was sending advance messengers of birds, wild roses, twining ropes of pink and white convolvulus. It was growing nearer every minute.

Suddenly there was a country stillness so deep it seemed to settle in drowsy layers like falling leaves. Ellen heard the whisper of hair across her shoulders as she turned in her seat.

The car had stopped. Her heart drummed in its cage of bone. She was afraid to open her mouth, afraid to break this enchanted silence with human speech.

Then Cass was babbling. 'We're here, Nell. Isn't it perfect? Isn't it the loveliest place you ever saw? I knew it! It's meant for us.'

'It's a school,' said bewildered Ellen, climbing out of the car in a daze.

MIDSUMMER HOUSE PREPARATORY SCHOOL said the weathered sign in front of her.

'It looks like a fairy-tale castle but it's a funny old school in the middle of nowhere.'

'But look at the towers,' sang Cass. 'And the view. You can see for miles, you can see the marshes. If you squint hard you can even see the sea. Isn't it incredible?'

Ellen didn't speak straight away. She wanted to be truthful.

She looked at the broken upstairs windows where swallows flew cockily in and out as if the house belonged to them. She saw the white roses smothering the walls and trying to poke their ramblers under the roof, and she noticed honeysuckle and starry vines of clematis crowding into the porch, so the estate agent had to drag them away in swathes before he could get the key in the door.

Then she followed Cass's rapt gaze across the water meadows to the marshes and the faint shining margin of the sea, as a pair of wild swans flew overhead uttering their hoarse sobbing cry, and she put her hand quickly into her mother's. Because she did see how beautiful it all was. She saw.

And she said honestly, 'Yes. Yes, it really is. It's lovely.'

Because she couldn't explain about the other thing, the terrible sadness that was here, the greater sadness that was coming to them.

Cass hugged Ellen hard. 'You stand on that step there, Nell,' she said, 'and I'll take your picture so your dad can see how wonderful this place is. Oh, he's going to *love* it.'

The estate agent peered out of the door, wondering why they weren't following him and Cass called, 'We'll have a good look round, don't worry. But I can tell you right away, we're going to take this house. It's what I've been looking for all my life. A dream come true.'

2

The Broken Angel

It was bitterly cold the night the baby was born but
Ellen couldn't settle by the fire. Instead she perched on
the window seat, between the eerie snowlight that
came through the uncurtained window and the golden
glow of the lamp.

She was flicking through a photograph album,
pulling a face at last year's picture of herself, grinning
like a loon, surrounded by a jungle of creepers. Then
she peered more closely, wondering uneasily if Cass's
camera had captured the persistent presence that had
dogged her steps that long summer's day.

Months had passed since then; months filled with
builders, plumbers, carpenters; countless journeys back
and forth between Suffolk and London. At last
Midsummer House was ready to move into. The
kitchen was exactly the kind of farmhousey kitchen
Cass had always wanted. The bathroom had the right
kind of bath with lion's feet, and the dining room had
the perfect table for dinner parties. The photo album
was Cass's record of the transformation of Midsummer
House. Cassie's Castle, Ellen's father christened it.

But Ellen thought it had looked most like a castle
that first day, sleepily smothered in roses and
honeysuckle, as if it was waiting for a prince to ride up,
clearing away the brambles with his sword. And there
had been a wild sadness in the air, she remembered. As

if someone or something was silently crying out to be rescued.

But that was before Midsummer House became a proper house for human beings again instead of a leaking sanctuary for birds, mice and beetles. It had been eerie, walking into the hall that first afternoon across the leaf-littered floor. Even for a few weeks after they moved in, whenever she turned a corner, or opened a door, Ellen had often felt she'd just missed a fleeting someone; someone shy and magical who had grown to love the house and was reluctant to leave.

Now the hall had a floor of highly polished wood. Paintings and hangings covered flawless ivory walls.

Ellen closed the album, knelt on the cushioned window seat and breathed on the cold dark glass.

Mrs Lumkin was supposed to be looking after her while the baby was being born, but there had been some trouble with one of her sons and she was late. The midwife had arrived an hour ago. Ellen's father let her in, white with nerves but pretending to be perfectly calm. He'd driven down from London as soon as Cass phoned to tell him the baby was coming.

Someone at her old school had told Ellen having a baby could hurt so much the mother died. But so far the noises floating downstairs sounded reassuringly like the sounds of hard work, with sudden bursts of excitement, reminding Ellen how Cass yelled aloud to see rockets on Fireworks Night or when she'd finished a drawing that had gone just right.

Ellen stared dreamily at the lamplit room bobbing outside in the winter garden. Now and then snow blew past in fine white veils, the room-in-the-garden vanished, and there was only the cold blueish light of the snow. Then the wind dropped again and the room magically reappeared. Cass had stayed up all one night

11

to paint this room dark rose and hyacinth blue. In the morning Ellen found her mother asleep with her head in the breakfast things, paint streaking her wrists and hair. When Ellen gently shook her she said, without opening her eyes, 'Hello, Nell, sweetie – Hey, I finished it,' and went on sleeping, smiling in her sleep.

Ellen's room was finished too. Cass had painted it in singing earth colours and had a special bed made for her that she had to climb up to. Ellen thought it was like sleeping high in a tree house in a beautiful orchard.

Cass hadn't yet found the time to do anything to her own bedroom. The walls were still bare hacked-about plaster, the floor splintered uncarpeted boards. When Cass knew the baby was coming today she'd hastily dragged the junk from around the enormous brass bed to clear a space. Even so the first thing Ellen's sister was going to see in this world was a jumble of ladders, rollers and tins of paint.

The baby's room had been ready for weeks. Cass had spent days shut in there by herself. But Ellen felt terribly uneasy when she saw what Cass had done. The strange little nest instead of a crib, the misty walls patterned with weeping trees, ferns, and rushy, flower-fringed pools. It was completely beautiful. The most beautiful room Ellen had ever seen. The leaves and flowers were so real it was like walking into a magic grove. But babies should have friendly rooms, Ellen thought, full of teddy bears, cheerful mobiles and Winnie-the-Pooh and Eeyore.

The builders and carpenters had driven the wild things from the rest of the house, shutting them out forever. But this small room was still somehow haunted with a sad sweet longing as if the house had stored all its old restlessness and yearning here, like wild honey in the comb.

12

Ellen's skin prickled. At the back of her mind a thin, bodiless voice was trying to warn her:

Swa – siss swa – siss.

She didn't want to sound critical, so she only said, 'Should all the baby's flowers be water flowers? Couldn't you paint a few land flowers too.'

Mrs Lumkin looked troubled, too, when Cass excitedly showed off her handiwork. Cass wanted her to admire the material she'd chosen for the curtains, but Mrs Lumkin told her she must leave a tiny corner of the hem unfinished when she sewed them. It was bad luck, she said, to have everything perfect before a new baby's arrival.

'Finish them *after* he's born,' she advised.

Mrs Lumkin always called the unborn baby 'he'. She had five boys, every one of which was a mortal worry to her, she said, and every one of whose names, Ellen had been fascinated to discover, began with an 'S'.

'I won't have time to do a thing when she's born,' laughed Cass, in the way that showed she was getting cross. 'That's why I'm working so hard now.'

Ellen could see Mrs Lumkin didn't approve of the baby's nighties either; long white pintucked ones fastening with silk ribbons that glimmered as if moonlight was magically sewn into them.

'Best buy half a dozen babygros, Mrs Carson,' Mrs Lumkin advised. 'They do them in lovely colours and they don't need any ironing. No sense making more work for yourself when you've a baby to care for.'

'These nighties are traditional,' Cass said stubbornly. 'I'll never have another baby, Mrs Lumkin, so I'm going to do it all perfectly this time.'

It was the day after she finished the baby's room that Cass took Ellen to visit the church on the cliff.

They'd been into Woodbridge for the shopping and

were almost home when Cass braked sharply at a crossroads and said, 'We never went to see the church, did we, Nell? We were going to go that day, but I was so excited about finding Midsummer House I forgot. Would you like to see it now?'

Ellen knew that as soon as they got back indoors Cass would shut herself away again with her paint brushes and stencils. When they first moved to Suffolk Cass took Ellen for long walks exploring the lanes and water meadows, the larch woods, the wild pebbly shore. But after a week or two Cass said she didn't have the time for any more excursions, because of having to get the house perfect before the baby came. Ellen wanted her mother to herself again for a while. So she said yes, she'd love to see the church.

'But what's so special about it?' she said as Cass drove them down a narrow, rather gloomy track.

'You'd know all about it if you'd let me show you round the museum,' Cass teased her, 'because it has masses of stuff in it about the history of this area. And you'd have found out that once, where we're going now, there used to be a big city, a port, in fact. One of the biggest in England in ancient times.'

'Where did it go?' asked Ellen uneasily. How could a whole city simply disappear? 'Did it burn down, like the fire of London?'

'No,' said her mum. 'And it wasn't the plague, either. It was geography that did for it in the end. In this part of the world the coastline changes terribly quickly. The land simply crumbled into the sea, Nell, and the city went under the waves.'

Ellen swallowed hard. Her shadow was hovering near again, just waiting to creep between her and the sun. Desperately she willed it away.

'How could it?' she objected anxiously. 'Did the sea

just whoosh in and drown the city? Did all the people die?'

She'd been right from the very beginning, she thought. This was the shining edge of the world. A place where streets, homes and children might suddenly vanish overnight.

'Not all at once,' said Cass, sensing her fright. 'Gradually, over several years. The cliffs and the houses on them slowly crumbled into the sea. The port silted up so the ships couldn't sail close enough any more and the people, well, they went away, I suppose, to find homes and work somewhere else. This is it, look. Not that there's much to see. Those little whitewashed cottages came along later, I'd imagine. But beyond them there's just the church and the cliffs.'

This was the loneliest place in the whole world, Ellen thought. Perhaps on a summer's day, when the grass was green and the air was warm, she might have thought it was beautiful, but today the bare clifftop and the empty windswept dunes below seemed unbearably desolate. For a moment she felt quite dizzy with fear, as if this was all there was, and all there ever would be; as if all the colours had ebbed from the world while she wasn't looking, leaving it lifeless, bleached as driftwood.

But the sky over their heads was blue, she noticed with relief, even in winter. Blue enough to hurt her eyes.

'That's the gravestone, look,' said Cass.

It was so ancient and weathered the inscription was completely worn away. It seemed strange that the stone itself had persisted so stubbornly through the centuries when it gave no clue what kind of man or woman had once been buried beneath it.

As Ellen peered cautiously over the crumbling edge

of the cliff, she saw a figure in jeans and headscarf striding along beside the lashing grey waves. Ellen knew who she was; she was Marsh Mary, and she lived like a gypsy in a shack where the marshes met the sea. Everyone said she was mad.

'I don't know why it is, but she doesn't have a civil word for any human, yet my Stephen saw her crying her eyes out over a seal she found dying on the rocks,' Mrs Lumkin had told her. 'Wild creatures are all she cares about, and if she finds one that's poorly she'll nurse it like it was a little old baby.'

If Marsh Mary was mad, her madness must be a harmless kind, Ellen decided sympathetically, if it made her care so tenderly for helpless creatures.

She followed Cass thoughtfully into the church. Rather a lot of it seemed to be falling down. The dangerous parts were propped up with scaffolding and roped off with signs warning sightseers to keep away. Through a rent in the roof Ellen saw the needle-like glint of a plane threading itself through the vault of blinding brilliant blue.

Inside the church she could still hear the sound of the wind and the pounding of the waves. A sparrow was fluttering against a pane of glass that was stained as blue as the sky. Snail trails waltzed across the worn stone floor. A complicated smell of rotten wood, mouldy prayer books, dust and paraffin filled the air.

It reminded Ellen of Midsummer House before the builders tamed it. A church for wild things, she thought, secretly picturing the congregation. Marsh Mary would be there, of course, a gull perched fiercely on her shoulder, seals, hares, stoats and foxes gathered bright-eyed at her feet, their strange voices joining with the pounding of the sea, and everywhere the soft radiance of thousands of candles . . .

16

'This is what I wanted to show you,' Cass said, breaking into her dream. 'I was afraid they wouldn't still be here after all these years. Look up, Ellen. Look up as far as you can.'

Ellen obediently craned her head so far back it hurt.

'Angels,' she said, awed.

A crowd of winged people smiled down from the worm-eaten timbers. Their chipped faces of faded rose and gold were calm, as if they didn't resent the alterations time and weather had made, their carved, gilded wings stiffly spread like the wings of eagles.

'The angels aren't all the same, Nell,' said Cass waiting for her to notice something. 'Look in the corner, behind those carved leafy bits.'

Ellen peered upwards through the gloom. Then she said, 'Oh, there's a child one, a baby, holding her big sister's hand. They don't look half so holy as the others, do they?'

Cass smiled. 'My guess is the woodcarver slipped them in amongst the others, thinking no one would notice. I think they were his own daughters, don't you? The bigger one reminds me of you with those eyes. "Wise beyond her years."'

She squeezed Ellen's hand. The phrase was a family joke. Granny Carson, Ellen's father's mother, had used it to describe Ellen, who had been furious. 'It makes me sound so boring,' she stormed. 'So goody-goody.'

'The littlest one looks too wild to be an angel,' said Ellen, rubbing her aching neck but unable to tear her eyes away from the angel sisters.

One of the baby's angel wings was so badly damaged it was hardly more than a stump, yet still she flew fiercely, unwavering, through the starry firmament, her hair a cloud of pale fire.

'She's got flowers in her hair,' said Ellen. 'And she

17

looks so sad and strange. As if all of her's not quite here.'

'She looks lonely,' Cass agreed. 'Like a nature spirit who's got mixed up with the angels by mistake. But don't you love her little face? Like a flower. I used to be glad she had that sensible big sister to take care of her. *She* looks altogether more down to earth, if angels can ever be down to earth. But then I was a freaky only child,' she said, laughing at herself. 'And I put all my troubles down to never having a sister to take care of me.'

Ellen felt a pang, remembering the sadness that was coming. She tucked her hand inside her mother's, tugging her gently towards the door, needing to be outside again.

'We'll have your sister christened here,' nattered her mother happily as they made their way back to the car. 'I'm sure we can persuade the vicar. Won't it be wonderful, Ellen! A real country christening.'

'Why are you always so sure it'll be a "her",' objected Ellen.

'Because I know,' said her mum. 'Because I've always wanted two daughters. Because I know you two will be friends and look after each other forever.'

She smiled dreamily, her hand briefly resting on the curve of the unborn baby, and Ellen knew she was seeing the angel sisters, flying hand in hand.

'Well, if she *is* a girl,' said Ellen, 'what are we going to call her?'

But Cass only answered maddeningly, 'I'll give you a clue. Until she's born, her name is a complete secret. Even your father doesn't know what she's going to be called. But I've hidden a clue somewhere in her room, so it's all safely ready and waiting for her.'

Ellen's skin prickled uneasily again. She had read

enough fairy tales to know that a baby's name was the spell the mother and father wove around it to keep it safe until the child could fend for itself. This was a piece of magic so old no one even remembered it was a spell any more; it seemed so humdrum, ordinary. But it was strong magic, Ellen thought.

Cass had her own brand of female magic, but by itself hers was a wild, lopsided kind. Ellen couldn't trust Cass to keep away the coming harm.

Now, listening to Cass's yells that were growing louder, more triumphant, and much closer together, she knew she was urgently needed upstairs.

She arrived outside the baby's room at the exact moment someone upstairs gave a surprised-sounding cough, followed by a silvery thread of a cry. Ellen stood with her hand glued to the door knob. For a moment she was unable to move, tingling from head to toe, her veins singing silver in sympathy.

Cass said something in a soft, excited voice, and Ellen heard the midwife say, 'We'll call your little girl in later. Let's just get the baby wrapped up warm.'

Quickly Ellen opened the door to the baby's room.

Moonlight, snowlight, streamed in through fluttering curtains. Cass had defied Mrs Lumkin and hemmed them both. But Ellen knew now how to keep the sadness away for a little longer. If she could only guess her sister's name . . .

'Fern?' she whispered experimentally. But not even Cass would call a baby Fern.

'Ivy?' she tried. 'Willow?'

Surely not. She searched the walls with their ghostly reeds and rushes, their weeping silvery boughs, dim floating flowers. She put on her glasses to bring the flowers more sharply into focus.

Water violets? It couldn't be Violet. Cass had lived

with a dreadful Aunt Violet in Lancashire for a whole year after her parents died. She still had nightmares about her.

Iris? Or Cress? Ellen had known a girl called Cressida at her old school. Marsh Marigold? That was worse than Marsh Mary.

Her father was calling. 'Ellen, where are you? Your mother wants to see you.'

'I'm coming,' she called, to give herself time. 'Just a minute.'

As she was despairing, she saw them; clusters of delicate ivory bells framing the alcove where Cass had placed the baby's bed; so they seemed to guard the odd little nest like glimmering sentinels.

Cass had listened to Ellen after all and painted lilies. Not rootless, floating water lilies but lilies of the valley, lilies of the earth.

'Lily,' Ellen whispered. 'My sister's name is Lily.'

'Ellen – don't you want to come and see your baby sister?' Her father was trying all the doors on the landing, looking for her.

'Coming,' she called again, excitedly and she was going to shout, 'I know her name, Daddy!'

Then she heard a commotion of wings, a chorus of hoarse voices high overhead.

At the same moment something small and white blew in across the windowsill, floated on the air for a second, then settled like a snowflake on the baby's nest.

'How strange,' whispered Ellen, and her skin broke out into goose flesh.

But she had guessed the name in time. She had spoken it aloud. Her little sister was safe now, anchored by root and stem, a child of the earth.

Ellen felt strong and full of hope. Because if she

20

could outwit the sadness once, she could do it again. Maybe she could even keep it away forever.

Ellen ran then, out of the moonlit grove of the baby's room, bursting gladly into the untidy lamplit place, where Cass waited, glowing, dishevelled, seeming not the slightest bit tired from her efforts.

And in her arms, wrapped in a little bloodstained blanket, was the tiny sister who had taken so long to arrive; wide awake, wondering, her drying hair a pale floss of gold, her eyes a kitten's milky blue. She gazed unblinkingly at Ellen, and made a creaking, thoughtful sound like an old door, her tiny starfish fingers fidgeting busily in the air.

'Hello Lily,' said Ellen. 'Hello little funny, creaky Lily. I think you need oiling.'

Cass beamed back at her. 'You guessed,' she said. 'I wondered if you would.'

'And I sort of named her, didn't I?' said Ellen shyly. 'The lilies were sort of my idea, weren't they?'

Ellen's father came back in the room looking worn out, saying, 'There you are, Ellen. I've been looking everywhere – Cass, did you mean to leave that window wide open in the baby's room? All sorts of rubbish was blowing in; old leaves and enough feathers to stuff an eiderdown.'

But Cass and Ellen took no notice; for staring fixedly at her big sister, Lily was solemnly fastening her fingers around Ellen's with the determined grip of a tiny vine.

'See,' said Cass, almost singing. 'Isn't she perfect? She loves you already.'

'And I love her,' said Ellen, her heart bursting. 'I love her too.'

Ellen's father smiled down at them, Cass, Ellen and baby Lily. 'My little family,' he said. 'All complete.'

Despite his tiredness, his eyes were softer, happier

than Ellen had seen them for a long time. Yet at his words a shiver ran through her as if someone or something was listening to them. Something that could still bring terrible harm to them all.

'Not quite complete,' said Cass critically. 'I'm in need of a very large plate of scrambled eggs on toast. I'm *starving*.'

Ellen's father laughed. 'Scrambled eggs at midnight!' he said. 'What a demanding woman you are.'

We've tricked it, we've tricked the sadness, Ellen thought, and she too laughed up at her mother and father, hugging them both hard, fierce in her happiness that the four of them were together at last, safely held in that charmed circle of lamplight. Nothing can hurt us so long as we all love each other. I won't let it.

3

Over the Edge of the Wo

'It will be the most amazing christening there's ever been in Suffolk,' bubbled Cass. 'People will tell their grandchildren in years to come. Mrs Lumkin's sister has put the finishing touches to this just in time. What do you think, Tom?'

Ellen's father had just driven down for the weekend. He looked up from his pile of papers.

'Taraa!' said Cass triumphantly.

She was holding a minuscule coat hanger from which an old-fashioned christening gown of silk and lace fell in dazzling flounces.

'There's a bonnet too,' said Cass. She waved a tiny lace-trimmed meringue, trailing ribbons. 'Don't you love them? I found them in an antique shop in Wickham Market. They just needed restoring to their original splendour.'

'Nice,' Ellen's father said, smiling his tired end-of-week smile. 'Very nice indeed.'

'Tom,' protested Cass. 'It's better than "nice".'

'It's absolutely lovely, Cass,' he agreed.

Ellen looked up from her crayoning. 'Lily won't like all those frills,' she said critically. 'She likes wriggling around with her nappy off.'

'Oh, you two,' sighed Cass exasperated. 'It's only for an hour. She won't have to wear it for *life*.'

There was a piercing wail upstairs as if Lily had

herself abandoned on a remote mountain
. . . Ellen and Cass had grown used to Lily's dramatic
way of announcing the end of her naps but Ellen's
father looked shaken each time.

'You were such a civilised baby, Ellen,' he said. 'I
don't think I've ever told you how much I appreciated
that.'

'I'll go, Mum,' said Ellen quickly. 'You talk to
Daddy. He's only just got here.'

'Careful coming downstairs, then,' Cass frowned.

'I always am,' said Ellen.

She flew to Lily's room, turning her name into a
song, the way she always did.

'Princess Li·ly, Princess Li·ly. Don't cry, Li·ly.'

By the time she reached her Lily was wildly
expectant, kicking her covers off like a tiny swimmer,
beaming her toothless smile.

'Ouf!' said Ellen, wrinkling her nose as she scooped
her out of her nest. 'You don't smell like a lily, Lily.
You smell worse than the chicken farm. Don't do that
when you're glammed up in your dress on Sunday, will
you?'

Lily's eyes sparkled. She leaned into her big sister's
shoulder, so that the top of her head nestled under
Ellen's chin, and began to make the cooing pigeon
sound that always made Ellen's heart turn over with
love.

'We just need some May sunshine,' said her father,
passing Ellen and Lily on the stairs, ruffling both their
heads. 'Then the christening will be perfect.'

'Well, Mum usually gets her way, doesn't she?' said
Ellen, grinning.

But her father didn't smile back. As she handed Lily
over to Cass Ellen felt a twinge of fear. It's because he's
tired from the long drive, she thought, after his hard

week at work. Things will be better when he lives with us again, the way he used to.

'We'll all be together soon,' Cass kept promising. 'We must try to be patient.'

But I miss him, she realised. I miss him all the time. And the missing went on, day after day, even when her father was with them. As if lately he wasn't with them in the right way. Wasn't really with them at all. When her father walked into Midsummer House this afternoon, throwing down his overnight bags, calling for Cass, Ellen had jumped with fright, spilling orange juice everywhere.

'I thought you were a burglar,' she confessed, when she'd recovered.

'A funny kind of burglar, announcing his arrival!' joked her father.

Later she'd had to show him how to work the new jug kettle. And where Cass kept the biscuits. As if he was a visitor.

If things had been normal he'd have known about other things too. She wouldn't have had to show him how to sing 'Row, Row, Row the Boat' when Lily was sad. He didn't understand about Lily's sad times. No one did except for Ellen. No one else ever seemed to notice the bewilderment which sometimes flitted across her sister's face as if she was straining to hear a voice calling to her from a long way off. Whenever Ellen saw that expression, fear dried her mouth, and for a few moments it was hard to breathe.

'It's only colic,' Cass said, when Ellen worriedly tried to tell her. 'Or wind. Most babies get a touch of wind from time to time. If you rub her back she'll soon feel better.'

But Ellen had discovered that only singing softly to Lily over and over would bring her blinking out of her bewildered trance.

'Your name is Lily,' Ellen would say to her fiercely, then. 'Lily Seraphina Carson. This is your home. And you belong here with us.'

The day before the christening, Ellen stopped by the door of her father's study. 'Would you like to go for a walk?' she asked wistfully. 'Mummy's busy getting things ready and it's lovely and sunny.'

He frowned, trying to hear over the stereo. Ellen's father liked to play loud Italian opera while he was working. He was scribbling in beautiful blue writing over large waxy sheets of paper. Ellen knew the sheets were plans for a new shopping centre. 'You know I'd love to, Ellen,' he said. 'Perhaps later. I've got to finish this before the relations arrive.'

Ellen stole away so as not to disturb him, and stepping under the canopy of budding honeysuckle went out alone into the sunlit morning.

She wasn't in the least sad, she told herself. Her father couldn't help being busy. When he lived with them properly again he would go for walks with his children, like other fathers. Today she would just have to go by herself. She'd go down to the water meadows, as far as the old windmill with broken sails, the furthest she'd yet been on her own. And this time she'd pluck up the courage to go down Dark Lane, past the cottage with twisty barley-sugar chimneys that once belonged to the village blacksmith. Raymond Molster told her a giant lived there now; a bearded giant, who ate out of tins with his bare hands and charged roaring after any children who dared to come near. Raymond was a liar, Ellen thought, and wanted to scare her.

Ellen didn't like the children in her new school. They made fun of the way she talked. She was a bookworm, they said, who had swallowed the dictionary and was far too boring for anyone ever to want to be her friend. As Ellen had never found it easy to make friends, even in London, she thought this was probably true. Something strange came over her when she was with children her own age. A kind of dreary frost. The friendly words she wanted to say dried in her mouth and instead stiff, awkward comments came creaking out. The way a girl would talk if she'd swallowed a dictionary. And, without consulting her, Ellen's body would grow stiff and pokerlike, her face replaced by a cold, unfriendly mask, even though inside her all the time was another Ellen bouncing around like a puppy simply dying for someone to throw it a stick.

But Cass was so convinced the village school was an improvement on Ellen's old one, Ellen couldn't bring herself to tell her mother she was as much a failure in Suffolk as she had ever been in London.

Yesterday, after school was over, Bonnie Molster, Raymond's sister, screamed across the road to Ellen, 'You're a snob – you really think you're something, Ellen Carson!'

But it was the weekend now. Ellen was free, pattering along the lanes, a blackbird carolling high in a tree, the sun warm on her back. Something might happen. Something wonderful that meant she'd never have to go to school again.

Suddenly she was running, her hair flying out, warbling nonsense to herself and before she knew it she was racing fearlessly down Dark Lane through the green tunnel of trees, carefully scanning the hedgerow for the stile. There might be rabbits in the water meadow. There would definitely be tadpoles. She should have put her wellies on.

She had a stitch suddenly, and slowed down just in time to avoid colliding with someone dragging a heavy

27

sacking-wrapped something out of the back of a battered red Renault van.

From a large gash in the sacking a female arm dangled whitely. Ellen's eyes widened in horror. It was Raymond Molster's giant. Lugging a body into his house! She turned to run, but it was too late.

'Good morning,' the giant said pleasantly, his voice rumbling from somewhere in his stomach.

He didn't look like a murderer, Ellen thought. He wore a huge red jumper decorated with moth holes and his bushy beard was streaked with grey, like the wild hair sprouting out of his head.

Seeing Ellen frozen, unable to speak, the giant added, puzzled, 'Are you all right?'

In a minute the giant would roar and chase her away, Ellen thought. She hoped her legs would obey her, not turn to cotton wool the way they did in dreams.

'I'm only Ellen,' she whispered. 'Sorry.'

She couldn't take her eyes off the dangling arm. He followed her hypnotised gaze.

'Oh *this*!' he laughed. His laugh was bigger and even more rumbling than his speaking voice. 'Did you think I was disposing of a corpse?'

She managed a nod. Surely no one would laugh about a murder? Unless the giant was even madder than Marsh Mary.

'It's a sculpture,' he explained. 'Mostly I work in bronze but sometimes when I need extra money I make stuff for gardens. Nymphs and shepherds, that sort of thing. I thought I'd sold this particular nymph but she's come winging back again, as you see. Are you from the new family at Midsummer House, only-Ellen?'

Ellen nodded again. She was wobbly with relief and feeling extremely silly at the same time.

'My name's Ellen,' she corrected. 'Not only Ellen. I forgot to put my glasses on. That's why I didn't see it wasn't a real body. My baby sister's being christened tomorrow,' she added, to change the subject. 'In St Aidan's Church, the one on the cliff.'

'I hear,' he said. 'It sounds a very grand event by all accounts.' His eyes twinkled. 'The whole village is ablaze with it. My grandson had a special name for that church,' he added. 'When he was little and used to stay with me.'

'What was the name?' asked Ellen. Her skin prickled suddenly.

'The church that belongs to the sea,' the giant recited carefully. 'Misha swore it was the name the sea birds called it. He used to drive his mother mad insisting he could tell what the animals in the zoo were saying, too. It all stopped once he went to school, of course. And I miss it. Though I doubt if even school will be able to make Misha completely ordinary.'

'The church that belongs to the sea,' repeated Ellen, still prickling, remembering the drowned city and how she'd been afraid Cass was bringing her to live at the shining edge of the world. 'I'd better go now,' she said. Then, finding sudden courage, she stammered, 'Raymond Molster said you chase children.'

'If Raymond Molster is the weasel-faced runt who sneaked over my wall last summer to steal my grapes,' said the giant heatedly, 'he is perfectly correct. And you can tell him I'll hang him up by his horrible little heels next time.'

Ellen was staring at the gloomy front of the smithy. 'I thought grapes didn't grow in England,' she said. Through smeary windows she glimpsed tall, dusty-leaved house plants, and the looming shape of what seemed a strangely lifelike but horribly mixed-up

29

creature with a greedy bronze beak and claws. She was glad she didn't have to live here. It would give me nightmares, she thought, shuddering.

'My back garden is south facing and very sheltered,' the giant was saying. 'Grapes thrive there. When they're ready, I'll bring some for your mother, if you like.'

And he raised his hand to Ellen pleasantly and, hoisting up his garden nymph again, carted her unceremoniously under his arm into his dark, enchanted house.

Cass had her way. The weather was perfect for Lily's christening. There was a breeze that snatched a few hats as the splendidly dressed friends and relations parked their cars on the cliff top but the sun shone so brightly that when Cass lifted Lily out of the car in her antique christening gown, she turned her face away, sneezing like a kitten.

St Aidan's was so full of gauzy white flowers that the little church immediately felt solemn and magical, Ellen thought, breathing in their faint honey fragrance.

The older aunts were nervous about the holes in the roof but Cass's designer friends were wildly impressed. Ellen heard her mother explaining about the drowned city to a beautiful young man in a pony tail, who had travelled down from London to be one of the godfathers.

Earlier Ellen had decided her mother wasn't enjoying the friends or the relations. Under her smile she seemed tired and slightly sad. But now she was glowing again, slender in her creamy silk suit. Ellen's father, looking handsome, was chatting away to everyone in the charming way he always used to when people came to their London flat for dinner. Everything

30

was going wonderfully, she thought.

Ellen sat between Mrs Lumkin and an aunt who wore something shiny that took up a lot of room. An atmosphere of expectancy was slowly building up. Mrs Lumkin adjusted her hat and straightened her skirt. The vicar came to hover by the font, clearing his throat.

Suddenly a figure burst through the church door and strode straight towards the vicar without looking either to the right or the left.

It was Marsh Mary, iron-grey hair streaming down her back. Despite the sunshine she wore an ancient coat of rusty black, so long and loose it flapped around her like wings, making her look like an angry crow. There were circles under her eyes as if she had been up all night. Her face was tearstained.

People began fidgeting in their seats, murmuring disapproval. Ellen stood up to see better but the shiny aunt pulled her down again.

Even before Marsh Mary was properly in earshot, the words were tumbling out of her mouth.

'They said I'd find you here,' she called. 'I know you're a busy man but if the church can't help the helpless, who can? The last cygnet died last night.'

The words seemed to hurt her as they left her tongue, as if they'd been burning inside her a long time. 'It can't be allowed to go on,' she cried. 'If we don't – '

The vicar touched her sleeve, gently interrupting. 'Mary,' he said. 'As you see we have a christening today. This is a terrible thing and I would like to help but you must come and see me about it later.'

Marsh Mary spun round in alarm. For the first time, it seemed, she took in the scene. Cass was on her feet, horrified, protectively holding her baby against her shoulder.

31

Marsh Mary closed her eyes, muttering, as if praying it was all a dream. But when she opened them to find the nightmare still going on, it was as if she suddenly saw herself through the eyes of the startled congregation, Ellen thought. A crazy old woman ranting about swans.

'I'm so sorry,' she whispered. 'I didn't – I've been up for nights nursing – you see – What must you think? I'll go now.'

'I think that would be better,' said the vicar. 'Come up to my house later, Mary.'

She shook her head silently, backing away down the aisle, before she turned and fled, slamming the heavy door in her distress.

Ellen's eyes stung. Stay, she wanted to say. You've got far more right to be here than we have. St Aidan's is the church that belongs to the sea and the wild things that live in and beside it. But one look at Cass's face told her it was no use saying anything aloud.

After Marsh Mary's interruption there was a good deal of embarrassed coughing and muttering. Cass fussed with the ribbons of Lily's meringue bonnet. Ellen's father stared straight ahead, as if nothing had occurred.

'Thank goodness for that,' sighed the shiny aunt. 'That dreadful woman. Completely mad.'

The service began at last. Hymns were sung. Words spoken.

Ellen didn't hear. She was using all her willpower to keep out another voice whispering other, warning, words.

Swa siss – swa siss . . .

She tried to concentrate on the calmly rejoicing faces of the angels overhead. But her eyes were drawn again and again to the littlest angel with the broken wing;

her birdlike bones, haunted elfin face. And still the voice warned:

Swa siss – Swa siss . . .

The godparents left their seats. Standing beside the font in the pool of sunlight which fell through the broken roof, they solemnly made their promises.

The vicar took Lily from Cass's arms. The baby's hazy eyes stared wonderingly around.

'I baptise you . . .' began the vicar.

His lips continued moving but no one heard his next words for at that moment the sky tore like an old sheet. A deafening scream blotted out all other sounds. Then the familiar thunderous roar. Through the broken roof the jets looked close enough to touch, streaking towards the sea.

'Flaming Yanks,' muttered Mrs Lumkin, looking shaken.

But Lily was terrified. She began to howl. Cass made soothing noises. The vicar stroked Lily's hair and jiggled her expertly but still she yelled. The godmother clucked. The godfather with the pony tail looked bored and examined his nails. For some moments the church vibrated with the dying screams of the planes like an enormous cello.

'I think we'll begin again,' the vicar suggested when he could make himself heard.

And apparently untroubled by Lily's bawling, he began again where he had left off.

But it was too late.

Already the hairs were slowly rising on the back of Ellen's neck.

The sound that joined the ancient words of the baptism was not like the deafening scream of the American jets. This soft painful throbbing seemed to trouble no one but Ellen. The air filling with a pulse, an insistent heartbeat that gradually became the unbearable beating of wings.

Some of the congregation glanced up curiously but seeing only two swans flying overhead, their necks stretched out, calling incoherently in their hoarse tongue, they went back to concentrating on the service.

Only Ellen waited for the swans' return, unable to take her eyes off the frantic parents circling above the church, uttering cries of grief. It was only Ellen who felt the terrible sadness that was rising now, out of the earth, out of the air, the sea.

'. . . baptise you . . .' continued the vicar without faltering. Lily had stopped crying so his voice rose easily above the commotion of the swans. The cry of the birds was a natural sound like the wind, or the waves pounding at the foot of the cliff, so no one was alarmed. Not even by the birds' final anguished drawn-out cry as the vicar pronounced, ' – Lily Seraphina.'

But Ellen understood and began to shiver.

She had failed to prevent it after all.

The sadness had slipped between her sister and the priest's words as an eclipse comes between the earth and its sun.

Bewildered, the baby craned her neck, trying to follow the sound as the swans turned, heading inland, uttering their desolate cry. For a moment her eyes were a blur of pain. She flung out her hands with a hoarse protest, scarcely human. Then she ceased to struggle, her face shockingly emptied, blank and remote as a tiny moon.

The grown-ups stood to sing the final hymn. Ellen stood with them, her legs obeying her like a puppet.

But even the words of 'The Lord's My Shepherd'

couldn't drown the whispering voice in her ear and, now it was too late, she understood what the voice had been trying to tell her all these months.

Swan sister, hissed the voice in her ear. *Swan sister. Swan sister.*

As soon after the christening as she could, Ellen crept away to be by herself.

The godfather with the pony tail caught her sliding away from the chattering guests, and tried to tease her, pretending he thought she was going to see her boyfriend. When Ellen furiously shook him off, no longer caring if she seemed rude, the shiny aunt, helping herself to more cake, remarked that it was only natural for Ellen to be jealous of the baby.

'She'll have to learn, like everyone else,' Ellen heard Granny Carson say sourly. 'I saw her sulking behind those spectacles because this little angel was the centre of attention for once.'

Ellen bit her lip hard, trudged on up the stairs on legs that were suddenly full of sawdust, carefully closed the door of her room, hauled herself up the ladder into her new bed, pulled the quilt over her head and burst into tears.

She sobbed until she thought her aching head would burst. Then she ran out of tears and fell asleep. When Ellen woke it was dark. Someone had dressed her in her night things without her knowing.

She lay still for a long time while the terrible afternoon replayed itself inside her head in jerky fits and starts like a home video. The more she thought about it, the more confused and frightened she became. For reasons she couldn't understand, her life had been hideously transformed into the cruellest of fairy tales. And in Ellen's story there was no helpful bird, or wishing ring, no friendly nut tree to make things all come right in the end. There was only Ellen.

After the christening Lily lay silently in Cass's arms, blankly gazing at her own fingers. No one seemed to think this was strange but Ellen. No one but Ellen could see what had happened.

'She's so good,' the shiny aunt kept saying to Cass. 'Isn't she a good baby, Mum?'

Why could only Ellen see that Lily was not good, or even placid, but lost, lost forever over the shining edge of the world . . .

When Ellen woke later it was to a storm. Water rushed along the guttering and warbled into drains. A high wind shrieked down the chimney, slamming itself against her sash window.

But through the storm came another sound. A soft throbbing of wings high over the house. Two inhuman voices calling the drawn-out syllables of a wild, inhuman name.

'No,' Ellen shouted desperately. 'No, you mustn't. She's not your child. She's *ours*. She's my sister, Lily Seraphina. *Don't* call her that.'

She slithered down her ladder and went skidding across the rugs on the polished landing to Lily's room. Lily was crying. But this was not the imperious human roar of the Princess of Midsummer House, demanding a dry nappy. It was a hopeless gnat-like drone and Ellen's blood ran cold when she heard it.

She longed to run to her parents then and tell them everything; the whispering voice, the dead cygnet, the grieving swans who wanted Lily to take their child's place. But she remembered her father's face, handsome and angry, as he waited for Marsh Mary to leave the church. She pictured her mother, bright and heedless in her silk miniskirt, and knew it would do no good.

'There's no one but me,' Ellen whispered, and

36

turning the door knob went into Lily's room.

The darkness was electric with terror. From somewhere in the room came frantic sounds, like the thrashings of a trapped bird. Ellen got herself panting through the force field of Lily's fear to the far side of the room and groped for the lamp switch, terrified of what she might find.

But all she saw was Lily, twisting and turning, her tiny face and body rigid with fear, her lids tightly sealed in sleep. No tears streaked the baby's cheeks. But the feverish droning went on and on.

'Li·ly,' Ellen called in a frightened whisper. 'Li·ly. Li·ly.'

She had no idea if Lily could hear her but still she softly sang her sister's name over and over again. After a while she saw something flicker across Lily's face. A moment later the baby girl gave a huge shuddering sigh.

'Li·ly. Li·ly.' Ellen comforted her. 'You're my little sister, Lily. Remember me? Ellen? You still remember, don't you?'

Though she didn't open her eyes, Lily stopped her dreadful insect's droning and her breathing became calmer.

'I love you, Lily Seraphina,' said Ellen, stroking Lily's pale wisps of hair. 'And I know you maybe can't remember who you are any more,' she went on, her voice wobbling. 'So I promise to remember for you until you get your real name back. And you will, I know you will. I'll help you do it somehow.' She scarcely knew what she was saying, just went on talking and soothing until she was sure Lily was asleep again. Then Ellen switched off the lamp and went back to her room where the storm still raged against her window.

For a few minutes she stood shivering in her pyjamas, staring in her dressing-table mirror in the half darkness. She could just make out the sharp knowing expression in her own dark blue eyes. Old beyond her years. Too clever for her own good. Snob. Bookworm. Swallowed a dictionary. You think you're something, Ellen Carson. But you couldn't stop this happening, could you?

'I'm scared,' she said aloud. 'And no one can help me.'

Then, as she climbed back into bed the voice began whispering again. The voice that knew, always knew, had always known, what was going to happen. The voice she had struggled so hard to shut out.

'*Three years and a day*,' it said. '*She will stay with you for three years and a day.*'

4

Earth Child, Star Child

Ellen was lying on her stomach crayoning, trying not to hear the telephone conversation in the hall.

'But it's her second birthday,' Cass was saying. 'It will be such a shame if you can't – I've ordered the cake, Tom. All her friends are coming to the party ...'

Ellen began to hum loudly. Her picture was coming along well, though it was hard to get the reflections on the water right. She licked her crayon, the kind that can be used wet or dry, carefully blurring the colours of the rainbow she had drawn arching over the meadows.

'Well, would you be able to come down the next day?' Cass said, her voice strained. 'We could postpone it if you – Oh, hello, sweetheart.' Her tone changed abruptly to a soft, infinitely patient one. Lily must have wandered into the hall.

'Do you want to go and find Ellen, darling. She's in the –'

'Lily,' called Ellen quickly. 'I'm here.'

After a few moments Lily arrived in the sitting room by degrees.

She didn't walk in directly but drifted in barefoot on delicate tiptoe, in a hovering, circling, uncertain way. Lily was a tiny, small-boned child, even for a two-year-old. She was so pale the light seemed to shine through her. Her fair curls gleamed around her small face like the pointed petals of a celandine. She looked frightened.

Suddenly Ellen's little sister grabbed hold of her own ears as if they hurt her, giving a shrill, birdlike screech. Lily couldn't bear quarrels, even unspoken ones. She picked them up out of the air like radio signals. And she could tell when people told lies however much they smiled. Only Ellen knew these things about Lily, but she had no idea what to do with what she knew.

'Li·ly,' said Ellen, her heart lurching as it always did. 'Li·ly. Don't get upset. It's OK.'

Lily put her hands down at once, smiling vaguely, without once looking at Ellen. Drifting to the window she clambered expertly on to the window seat where she squatted, rocking on her haunches.

'Twinkle twinkle little star,' she sang in her pure, clear voice. Her eyes scanned the ceiling. She stretched out her hands, looking upwards through thin, translucent fingers, giggling as if she saw welcoming beings, magic birds perhaps or talking animals, where Ellen saw only paint and wallpaper.

'. . . little star . . .' Lily repeated. She only ever sang those few words of the rhyme but they gave her enormous pleasure. Ellen's sister had never spoken a word, yet she could *sing* several words perfectly. Ellen often sang the words back to Lily, changing them slightly, making a game of it. It was the only game she could share with her now, the only way she could reach out to her without frightening her away. She did it now, softly calling on two notes: 'Earth child, star child . . .'

Sometimes when Lily got upset she scarcely seemed a human child at all, but more a tiny troll. But when her sister was in this sweet dreamy mood, Ellen could make herself believe Lily really was a child who had

40

been sent to this planet by mistake. Perhaps somewhere in the universe was a distant star where the people sang to each other instead of using speech, and where they knew the thoughts of all living creatures, visible and invisible.

'But it's her second birthday,' Cass yelled in the hall, at the end of her tether now. 'She'll be two years old. How *dare* you be too busy for your own daughter, damn it.' She slammed down the phone.

Lily flung up her hands, wailing, pulling furiously at her hair. 'Aaaah,' she droned tearlessly, her face expressionless. 'Aaaah, aaaah.'

Cass came running immediately. 'Oh, sweetheart, don't cry. You'll have your party. All your friends are coming. And there's going to be a big, beautiful cake.'

Ellen scrumpled up her first drawing and started again. 'Lily never eats cake,' she said angrily. 'You still feed her baby mush with a spoon.'

And she doesn't have any friends, she thought. Except maybe invisible ones.

But she couldn't say these cruel words out loud. And if she did, her mother wouldn't hear them. It was as if Cass was under a spell too and still saw the perfect child she'd always dreamed of.

Even Mrs Lumkin couldn't bring herself to tell Cass she suspected something was wrong. The nearest she got was to suggest Lily should have a hearing test because she was slow to talk.

But Cass said brightly, 'Don't be silly. Lily's hearing is perfect. Children do things in their own time. She learned to walk months earlier than other children. She'll talk when she's ready. Einstein didn't say a word until he was three.'

Now, peering down critically at Ellen's new

41

drawing, Cass balanced Lily across her hip. 'Lily loves parties,' she crooned, kissing the top of her little daughter's head. 'She's going to have a wonderful birthday, just like she did last year. Your daddy will come after all,' she told her. 'You'll see.'

Lily smiled briefly at her fingers. 'Little star,' she sang uncertainly, but next moment she began pulling violently at her own hair as if it belonged to someone else, a troll baby again.

Ellen crayoned black and purple thunder clouds crackling with forked lightning, and a splintered uprooted tree falling in slow motion before she answered painfully, 'Lily doesn't care a hoot about her birthday. It's you that wants it, Mum.'

But Cass had whisked into the kitchen to make jellies and fairy cakes and the other ingredients of another perfect birthday party for her little girl, giving no sign she'd heard a single word.

Ellen's father came home for Lily's party after all. He looked like a desperate ghost and hardly said a word. But Cass just chattered away, smiling more radiantly than ever. As if she believed she could shine brightly enough for both parents, Ellen thought.

The little girls arrived in their party dresses clutching gifts. Ellen wondered where Cass had found them all. But then Cass wasn't like Ellen. She didn't freeze in front of strangers or grow tongue-tied. She glowed. She bloomed. She told hilarious stories and people warmed to her at once. Even when Cass had to go to the dentist's in Framlingham she'd have made two new friends by the time she came out of the waiting room. Watching her greet each child by name as if it was the one person Cass needed to complete a perfect occasion, Ellen wondered glumly if perhaps she had been given to the wrong mother at birth.

The party seemed to go on for a painfully long time to Ellen. Lily tiptoed around amongst the pretty wrappings and discarded ribbons with a sweet, remote expression on her face while Cass exclaimed, 'Oh, isn't this lovely, Lily. Say thank you to Naomi. Now let's play Pass the Parcel.'

When the baffled small guests departed at last, Ellen crept into the winter garden to be alone. Far across the marshes were the brooding towers of the power station, outlined in harsh orange lights. Lately men worked all through the night, doing some kind of emergency repairs. When the Carsons first bought the house, a line of ancient trees screened the dark towers from view, but in recent months something had mysteriously infected them. Now the gaunt trunks stood stripped of their bark and branches, like trees struck by lightning.

Last year on the night of Lily's birthday the swans had flown over again, calling to her in their sobbing tongue. Her little sister had been inconsolable, crying wildly until the dawn, when she slept at last from sheer exhaustion.

Don't, Ellen prayed, please don't let them fly over tonight.

Each time the swans came, calling Lily's wild swan name, Ellen knew they lured her further from her human self, her human family, tightening the enchantment they had cast at Lily's christening.

That night Ellen kept a lonely vigil in her tree-house bed. She tried to read to take her mind off things but still plainly heard the downstairs clock chiming every hour.

Then it came like sudden rain. The beating of wings. The yearning voices. And the high thin voice from her sister's bedroom, joining theirs in pain and longing, weeping without words, weeping without tears.

Ellen ran to her room, gathered up the blank, shuddering little girl in her arms, and cried angrily, shaking her, 'You are my *human* sister, not my swan sister. You don't belong to them. You're our little girl, Lily, but you don't remember, do you? You don't remember!'

Then she jumped guiltily.

Cass stood in the doorway, astonished at finding Ellen there before her. 'Lily's having a bad dream, sweetheart,' she said tiredly. 'I'll take care of her. You go back to bed.'

Her mother looked so normal standing there in her nightie, her hair tangled, her face crumpled with sleep, that it suddenly seemed stupid to go on trying to bear this terrible nightmare alone. If Ellen explained properly Cass would understand. She must. Together they'd save Lily. The voice had said she would live with them for three years and a day. So they had a year. A whole year to work something out.

'Mum, she wasn't having a bad dream,' said Ellen urgently. 'It was the swans. They fly over our house and call to her the night after her birthday. They came after the christening too. She understands what they're saying. Mum, I think Lily thinks she belongs to them. She doesn't know she's our baby any more. She was *your* dream child, Mum, and now she's theirs. She can't help it. They've bewitched her with sadness. They took her name at the christening, and gave her a swan name instead and – '

'I think you must have a temperature, Ellen, you're rambling, sweetie.' Cass pitched her voice calmly and matter of factly above Lily's desolate cries. 'Or maybe you've been dreaming too. Pop back to bed and let me worry about Lily. She's had too much excitement for a little girl, that's all. I'll make her a warm drink and she'll be fine.'

Ellen unwillingly took her arms from around her baby sister.

'You *wanted* me to take care of her to begin with,' she said slowly. 'Before she was born. You showed me the angel sister, remember? That's how you wanted it to be. But now she's here you don't want anyone to love her but you. And there's something terribly wrong with her but you just won't see – ' She faltered. She had never seen this particular expression on Cass's face before but there was no doubting it was very angry indeed.

Ellen stood up quickly, scared, defeated.

'OK, sorry. I'm going. Goodnight,' she muttered.

'But there must be something I can do before next year,' she whispered, as she waited for sleep to come. 'In the story the girl makes shirts out of nettles and when the swans put them on, they get changed back into her brothers.'

But in that story the swan brothers knew they were enchanted and at night they always returned to their human form. That was a hundred times easier to deal with than the enchantment that had befallen Lily. I'd make Lily a nettle shirt if it would do any good, though, thought Ellen. I'd make a dozen. I'd do anything at all if it would save her.

Then the voice spoke firmly and distinctly. It seemed to be getting clearer, Ellen thought, puzzled.

If you have courage, follow the signs, it said.

'What do you mean?' asked Ellen aloud. 'Follow which signs? Why do you keep on telling me this stuff? Who are you? Where are you?'

She was bolt upright now, her skin prickling all over.

45

But as if it was a tape that could only play one recorded message at a time, the voice merely repeated meticulously:

Follow the signs. Follow the signs.

5

Enchanted

But after the night of Lily's second birthday Ellen's voice was bewilderingly silent. And as the weeks and months went by it became too easy to behave, like Cass, as if nothing out of the ordinary had happened in the Carson family. That everything was just as fine as it could be.

Besides, as time passed, the world of school took most of Ellen's energy. To escape her loneliness she found herself spending even more time reading and doing homework. If her teacher didn't give her any, she invented some for herself. The harder she worked the less the other children liked her. The less they liked her the harder she worked. It was like being trapped on a factory conveyor belt. Even if she wanted to she daren't get off. If she did she might have time to think . . .

After Lily's party Ellen's father came less frequently at weekends. He was busier than ever nowadays, it seemed. When he did come he spent long hours in his study working.

Ellen was shocked at how unhappy he looked when she saw him, briefly, at mealtimes. She knew he was in some kind of trouble. Something was wrong with a building he had helped to design years ago and people were angry with him. But when Ellen asked him about it, longing to sympathise, he told her sharply she was far too young to understand.

Cass, on the other hand, did less and less. After the move to Suffolk, she had continued to work as a freelance designer. And for the first months of Lily's life she'd gone up to London now and then to keep up with things and plan new projects. But lately all Cass seemed to do was look after Lily. Even though Lily needed so frighteningly little looking after.

Some days Ellen came home to find Cass by the fire, rocking Lily in her arms, humming lullabies, the two of them apparently in the same position they had been in when she left in the morning. And her mother would jump guiltily and say, 'Is that the time? I had no idea.' As if the interminable day Ellen had struggled through at school had passed in the space of a dream for Cass.

'Let's go for a walk, Mum,' Ellen would say then. 'Lily's too pale and it's so stuffy in here. Mrs Lumkin says she needs more fresh air.'

But Cass usually had an excuse to stay by the fire. Lily had a cold. Cass was tired, or expecting an important phone call. It was true Lily often had colds and that Cass, who used to be so lively, always looked exhausted these days. But almost no one phoned Cass any more. Her London friends were getting used to life without her. And her Suffolk friends, mostly other mothers with little children, had gradually stopped coming for long gossips over cups of coffee. Lily's strangeness, increasingly obvious now she was older, had frightened them away, Ellen thought angrily.

Ellen was used to walking to and from the village school on her own most days. But one autumn afternoon, to Ellen's surprise, Cass was waiting for her in the car when she came out. She was wearing eye make-up as she used to, and she'd had her hair done for the first time for ages. Lily, strapped in her car seat, dreamily examining her fingers, was wearing a velvet dress, green as spring moss.

'Is something wrong?' asked Ellen, alarmed.

'I've been shopping in Ipswich and now I'm taking my two lovely daughters out to tea,' said Cass. 'What's wrong with that?' And smiling so brightly Ellen could hardly stand to look at her, Cass drove them to Aldeburgh very fast, talking all the way.

They had a blowy walk along the seafront to inspect the ancient Moot Hall, which had originally been built three whole streets away from the shore, Cass told her. But after a while the October wind made Ellen's ears ache. They took refuge in the bookshop for half an hour or so where Ellen carefully chose some new paperbacks. And at last they went for tea in the Minsmere Tea Rooms, which was part of an old-fashioned hotel.

A frail, white-faced old man in a frighteningly grand waiter's uniform guided them silently across miles of carpet to a table beside an open fire. Ellen wondered if the waiter had been a young man when the hotel was built and watched anxiously as he toiled back to the kitchens. He was so thin he looked brittle, as if he were made of peppermint candy. Ellen tried to remember the name of the sweetshop owner in *Mary Poppins* who so gruesomely broke off her own barley-sugar fingers for the children to eat.

'Real linen,' said Cass approvingly, rubbing the tablecloth between finger and thumb. 'And beautiful old beams. I hope the cakes are as good as everything else looks here.'

Mrs Corrie, thought Ellen, with as much relief as if she'd extracted a splinter. That was it. The one with the galumphing great daughters.

She looked warily around her. Taking her sister to

public places wasn't always comfortable, but there was only one other family in the tea rooms so far and they were too busy quarrelling, she realised, to notice Lily tiptoeing eccentrically between the tables.

Strangely, although arguments usually upset Lily, this quarrel, loud though it was, didn't seem to bother her in the least. This family seemed to be enjoying its battle, Ellen noticed, amazed; each person trying to outdo the others in insults and witticisms. Gales of laughter reached Ellen's table.

Cass raised her eyebrows at Ellen and grinned, amused.

'Oh, those do look good,' she said greedily as the elderly waiter unloaded their order with trembling hands. 'And there's extra hot water for the tea. I love it when places do that.'

Ellen tucked into the scones. 'It's nice here,' she said. 'I'm glad we came.'

'So am I,' said Cass, spooning on jam and cream. 'We must do it again. It's time we bought you some new dresses too, Nell. Let's have a proper day out together soon. I never mean to get into a rut, sweetie, but somehow lately it sort of creeps up on me.'

Ellen looked away. This was the closest Cass had ever come to saying she had been unhappy. And though Ellen knew it was true, she also knew that by tomorrow Cass would be sorry she'd even hinted at it. But it was so lovely to see her out of the house, lively and smiling again almost like the old days. Perhaps Cass was nearly over her depression now, Ellen thought hopefully, the way people got over flu.

'I don't need another dress, Mum,' she said. 'But if you want to take me somewhere I'd like to go to Framlingham Castle. Or the otter sanctuary.'

With alarm Ellen noticed that one of the sisters in

the other family was yelling good-humouredly at her mother now. She couldn't imagine shouting at Cass who, in her own way, seemed recently to have become as fragile as the peppermint waiter. Ellen stole a quick look from under her brows. They look a bit foreign, she decided. Perhaps that explained it.

The one silent member of the family was a boy not much older than Ellen. He was dark like his sisters, with the same fine cheekbones and thick, dark brows, but he seemed to occupy less space than they did somehow. As if he didn't expect, or even want to be noticed, she thought. He had eaten only a mouthful of his cream cake and was drumming absently on the table as though he'd forgotten where he was. Lily, fascinated by the sound, circled tentatively closer to the boy's table, her thin fingers semaphoring away.

'It's all very well for you to tune us out like that, but it's you we're thinking of, Misha,' another sister cried suddenly in an exasperated voice. The boy smiled silently as if he was used to this kind of attack but Lily veered off in alarm, ducking her head, moaning and covering her ears.

Ellen jumped too. She had heard that name before.

Then a familiar bearded figure came into the room, clearing his throat, peering shortsightedly around him.

My giant, she thought. Of course, Misha's his grandson! And she realised she had secretly been hoping to meet this boy ever since his grandfather had told her about him.

'You might have brushed your jacket, Dad,' said Misha's mother fiercely, standing up to kiss her father, swatting irritably at his clothing with a jangle of her gold jewellery. 'You're covered in dust.'

'Sorry I'm late,' he said vaguely. 'I was just trying to finish – '

'Don't tell me,' sighed his daughter. 'You haven't changed a bit, have you?'

'I should hope not,' he joked. 'I was absolutely perfect to begin with.'

Ellen watched under her lashes as the giant hugged and kissed his grandchildren, pulled out a chair and sat on it as cautiously as if it was dolls' furniture.

Misha went back to his drumming. Lily circled closer. The drumming changed rhythm, speeded up, teasingly slowed down again.

He knows Lily's there, Ellen thought. He's playing a game with her. And she wondered if Misha had noticed her, too.

Unlike other people Misha didn't seem embarrassed by Lily's blank face or birdlike movements. Without seeming to, Misha had been talking to her little sister ever since they came in. Talking without words.

'Little star,' breathed Lily, hovering just behind his elbow, still ready to take flight if necessary. And Misha smiled, without once looking up at her as if he knew directness would frighten her.

How could the giant's grandson know Lily so well, Ellen wondered as Cass drove them home. How could he possibly know? The giant himself had greeted Ellen warmly as they left the tea rooms. 'Why, it's only Ellen,' he said. 'I didn't recognise you sitting over there. I never remembered to bring your mother those grapes, did I?'

'But that's Jack Kelly,' Cass had said excitedly, as soon as they were out on the street again. 'He's a well-known sculptor. How ever do you know him?'

'He lives down Dark Lane,' said Ellen. 'And he's a kind of friend of mine.' She smiled to herself. It wasn't often that she could impress Cass.

That evening she settled down contentedly on her

52

bed to read one of her new books. The description on the back was promising. A lonely girl kept an imaginary pony on wasteland where factories had been pulled down, near her home. One day, after a family quarrel, she ran away to this place and found a real pony identical to the one she'd imagined, apparently waiting for her, tossing its mane . . .

The story kept her engrossed until bedtime, but as Ellen was turning out the light she noticed the author's photograph inside the cover. An unsmiling woman with blazing eyes stared back at her. She was younger then, but still unmistakable. Marian Marshall, the author of *Dream Pony*, was Marsh Mary, the woman who loved wild birds and hated humans. Ellen was sure of it.

Next day everything went wrong. Cass looked dreadful at breakfast time. Lily had woken in the night, running a high temperature. Cass had been sitting with her for hours, sponging her, trying to calm her down.

'She's still very feverish. I'll have to ring the doctor,' she said. She seemed frightened, almost guilty as if she was worried about more than Lily's fever.

When Ellen came home from school Lily was uneasily asleep on the sofa. The doctor had only just left and Cass was crouching by the fire in tears. Cass hadn't taken Lily to the doctor's for months, it turned out. Nor for the usual check-ups to be weighed and measured. Not for her vaccinations. And when the doctor saw Lily she expressed concern. Not about the fever, which was only a common virus that was going round the village, but about Lily herself, her lack of speech, her unusual behaviour.

'But there's nothing *wrong* with her,' Cass wept angrily. 'How *dare* that woman say there is. Plenty of children are slow to talk. Lily's just shy. She's intelligent and sensitive, I know she is. Look how she loves music. She sat through a whole Mozart concerto with her ear to the stereo, and didn't move a *muscle*. Does that sound like a handicapped child to you?'

'I don't think Lily's exactly handicapped,' Ellen began timidly. 'I think she's been –'

'Do they think I'm going to subject my little girl to those terrible tests, as if she was some kind of scientific *specimen* –'

' – enchanted,' Ellen battled on. 'Enchanted by sadness. We've still got a few months left until her birthday. I think we could stop it together, Mum, if –'

'Oh, God – what on earth am I going to say to your father?' Cass burst out. 'Not that he really –'

Ellen felt her stomach lurch. *Don't say it*, she willed, but Cass stopped herself, blinking away her tears.

'My goodness, look at the time, Nell,' she said, as if nothing whatever had happened. 'I must get your tea. You'll be starving.'

'I'm not hungry,' said Ellen. 'Really.' This was true. She felt extremely sick.

'Don't be silly,' said Cass. 'You're growing and you must keep your strength up. Come in the kitchen and talk to me, sweetheart, while I scrub potatoes. Did I hear you mention Lily's birthday? What shall we buy her this time, Nell? Hasn't the time flown? It seems only the other day she was a tiny thing in a shawl –'

Hopelessly Ellen trailed into the kitchen.

It was not only Lily who was enchanted by sadness, she understood now, watching her brightly chattering mother begin efficient preparations for the meal neither of them would have the heart to eat. It was Cass, who'd been running from her own unhappiness ever since she was a little girl. But in the end, by some mysterious magnetism, that sadness had sought her out, drawing her slowly but surely to itself. Recently, for weeks at a time, Cass had given in, letting herself slide into that strange, sleepwalking apathy. But the more she fought to break out of it and be her old self again, the harder she struggled to leave that drowning pain behind, the tighter the poisoned web was drawn around them all.

The swans' enchantment was almost complete.

6

The Dark Tower

Christmas was over. Ellen's father came down on Christmas Eve and drove straight back to London on Boxing Day. Ellen knew part of the reason for leaving so quickly was the trouble he was having at work.

'I wish I could help you, Daddy,' she said wistfully, as she kissed him for the last time through the car window. Cass had taken Lily back indoors so she wouldn't catch cold again. For the first time for a long while her father really smiled at her. A sad smile, but real.

'So do I, sweetheart,' he said, squeezing her hand. 'But you just look after yourself. See you again soon.'

He started the engine.

'Will you come down for Lily's birthday, Daddy?' she called. 'I wish you would.' But he was driving off. She couldn't tell if he had heard her.

'Oh, I do wish you would,' she whispered. For somehow she felt the catastrophe might still be prevented if both her parents were at Midsummer House on Lily's third birthday. If they could all be together again in a charmed circle of light, the way they were the night Lily was born.

She couldn't bear to go back into the house. She didn't want to see her father's presents which had looked so exciting in their wrappings under the tree but seemed, once she had opened them, as if they were really meant for someone else.

She didn't want to go back into that too-warm living room and see Cass rocking Lily in her arms, with the bleak expression she almost always wore these days. There had been no more days out after all, since the trip to Aldeburgh. As if Cass thought Lily's illness was a punishment for trying to be happy again.

'I'm going for a walk,' Ellen called to her mother, grabbing her jacket from its hook in the cloakroom.

She felt as if she'd been trapped indoors for at least a year. Once upon a time her mother and father had liked to do things, go for walks, have friends for dinner, play games with Ellen. Once when she was very small she had dressed them up as king and queen, in velvet curtain robes and gold paper crowns. Her father was the King of the Sun and Cass the Queen of the Moon and they had lived inside a charmed circle of light. Once upon a time. Long, long ago . . .

She trudged off with her hands in her pockets, without the slightest idea of where she was going. Her legs had suddenly discovered a mind of their own.

It was a beautiful afternoon, clear amd sharp. The light would be gone in an hour or two. In the west the enormous sky was already deepening to sorbet colours; mainly raspberry ice, she decided, with swirls of purplish blackcurrant.

After the imprisonment of Christmas, walking lifted her spirits and unmuddied her thoughts, turning them clear, simple as the winter air. She couldn't imagine living anywhere else but Suffolk now. And today the strange sadness she often felt tugging at her, beneath the surface of the landscape, seemed to have ebbed away like a tide. Snowdrops poked their spikes through the mossy banks. The late afternoon light caught a yellow splash of winter jasmine on a wall.

Nothing bad is ever going to happen to Lily, she vowed. I just won't let it. And on such a day, with spring already exploding from every bough in tiny varnished-looking buds, it seemed impossible that any harm could come to her.

Then, as she passed a gap in the hedge, Ellen glimpsed two hares boxing crazily on their hind legs, like cartoon animals, right in the middle of the frosty cabbages. She laughed with surprise. Panicking at the human sound, the hares dropped back on to all fours, streaked through the cabbages, and over the raw red furrows of a recently ploughed field in a blur of flying paws and ears.

'You've hurt their pride,' said a voice behind her. 'They were taking it very seriously.'

Misha was grinning at her, beside the glossy green of a holly bush, his face glowing with the cold, his collar pulled up around his ears.

'You made me jump,' Ellen said breathlessly. 'You look like a tree spirit standing there. As if you just came whooshing out of the holly.'

The boy laughed. 'If I was a tree spirit I'd try to choose a more comfortable tree to live in! You were in the tea rooms at Aldeburgh, weren't you?' he added. 'While they were all deciding my fate.'

They seemed to have fallen into step, heading together towards Dark Lane and the water meadows.

'Your fate?' said Ellen, still recovering from her surprise. 'What do you mean. Who was?'

'My mum's gone off to America. On a tour with my sisters. They're musicians. Good ones. Not amateurs like me. The school I was at before didn't want me much because I'm no good at school things. So Mum asked my grandfather if he'd have me until they came back.'

'And he said "yes",' said Ellen, her heart leaping. 'Are you living here now?' She turned red then, realising how pleased she sounded. It would be awful if Misha was nice just because he felt sorry for her in her freakishness, her loneliness.

Yet Ellen, who had not yet learned how to make friends her own age, already mysteriously thought of Misha as her friend. A boy she could talk to without growing stiff and frozen like a human icicle; a boy who wouldn't jeer about snobs and dictionaries.

But he simply nodded and said without fuss, 'I'm here until the summer, I think. So if you'd like a temporary friend –'

Giddy with amazement that this elusive magic had suddenly worked for her after all these years, Ellen could only nod shyly.

You see, that didn't hurt too much, she told herself. You've got a friend. A real temporary friend.

They had reached the stile. 'It's muddy over the meadows if you haven't got wellies,' he said doubtfully. 'Would you like to come and meet my granddad instead.'

'I thought your grandfather was a giant,' she remembered. 'I thought he'd murdered someone. But he said it was only a garden nymph.'

They laughed.

'Granddad, a murderer – you're joking,' Misha grinned. 'My mother and sisters trample over him. He's as soft as anything. All his fierceness goes into his sculpture.'

'I saw some through the window when I was little,' agreed Ellen. 'All beaks and claws. It scared me.'

'We'll go round the back,' said Misha. 'He's just made some bread if you're hungry. His cooking is mainly awful. I'm getting so thin I'm in danger of disappearing.' He hammered on his ribs, which looked fairly well-covered to Ellen. 'But his bread is nice in a chewy sort of way,' he added. 'If you plaster loads of honey on it.'

Which was how Ellen found herself sitting at a scarred trestle table which looked as if it once belonged to Vikings, happily eating porridgy bread with honey, the runny kind, from a battered wooden plate which also seemed designed for warriors.

Jack Kelly's house was the strangest place she had ever been in, Ellen thought. Under the table her feet bumped unexpectedly into a large cardboard box, leaking spikes of straw.

'Methuselah's hibernating in there,' Misha explained. 'He's a very old tortoise. Really ancient.'

Ellen wondered if the tortoise had been called Methuselah when he was a baby reptile, but Misha wasn't sure.

'I suppose he may have been called Geronimo then!' he suggested and they both got the giggles.

'The one and only racing tortoise,' said Ellen spluttering. She hadn't laughed properly for ages, she realised. The thought made her curiously shy.

In front of Ellen on a dusty windowsill were several plaster casts of human faces, their expressions unnaturally calm, their pale, lashless eyelids eerily closed.

Beside her on the kitchen worktop was a jumble of sharp tools, tangled string, rubber moulds, a loaf with several slices sawn off it and an open tin of catfood.

The cat, Pushkin, was ancient like the tortoise. Striped like a tabby tiger, with enormous tired dark eyes, he lay on top of the central heating boiler with his paws dangling wearily down, and his mouth slightly open, as if he was on the verge of saying something extremely deep.

Cass would hate this cottage, thought Ellen, remembering how finicky her mum had been about getting things perfect at Midsummer House before Lily came. This was the messiest kitchen she'd ever seen. Misha would be lucky to reach next summer without getting food poisoning.

But she felt oddly comfortable. She could say what she liked here, and no one would mind, or be hurt. She'd had to be painfully careful at home lately. As if everyone in her family was made of expensive china and might break if Ellen didn't look after them.

'More bread, Ellen?' said Misha's grandfather cheerfully. 'Misha's always rude about my cooking. I don't know why. I make a cauliflower cheese that would make the angels weep.'

'That's true,' said Misha, rolling his eyes. 'That's because they'd all have violent indigestion.'

Ellen choked with alarm. She let her crust fall back on to her plate, ready to bolt for home immediately if necessary

But Misha's grandfather, who was clearly not the breakable kind, went on mildly wandering in and out in his dusty work clothes, hunting for a chisel. ('Sure you didn't bake it into the loaf?' Misha suggested.)

And Misha talked. Ellen had never met a boy who talked so much. He had been unnaturally silent in the tea rooms, she remembered. He told her about his family, whom he mainly liked, and the schools he had gone to, which he mostly hated, and the teachers who hated him.

'I can't read very well. There's some sort of problem apparently but I don't think I'm actually completely stupid or anything,' he said calmly. Then he talked about his father who worked abroad, wherever there were disasters, organising relief operations.

'But we haven't really lived with him for a long time,' said Misha. 'So it doesn't make much difference, him going away. He phones sometimes but it's mainly impossible to hear. Like having a conversation underwater.'

'My dad lives in London mostly,' said Ellen. 'But when we moved down here we thought he wouldn't.'

They were silent for a while, then Ellen said tentatively, 'Misha's not a very usual name.'

'It is in Russia,' said the boy, grinning. 'It's short for Michael. My dad was half Russian. Mum's part Italian and Granddad's half Irish. And somewhere there's some Persian, I think, or maybe it's Turkish, though I can't remember how it happened. Anyway that's why we all look a bit Arabian Nightsish. My sisters really revel in all that. Have you finished eating? Do you want to look round?'

'I mustn't be long,' said Ellen. 'Or Mum will worry.' But she badly wanted to stay. She had never met anyone like Misha in her life. She couldn't even have imagined anyone like him. She wondered how he'd get on with Raymond Molster and the others but Misha told her he wouldn't be going to school in the village. 'My granddad is going to teach me at home.'

'I wish he'd teach me too,' Ellen sighed jealously. 'I hate school so much.'

Fascinatedly she followed him from room to room. Misha's grandfather collected strange things as well as sculpted them, she noticed. Bowls and baskets full of intriguing objects; wooden eggs, unusual stones and fossils, some especially creepy things that looked like ancient withered mushrooms.

'Oh, yuck, that's a skull,' she said, snatching back her hand from a dusty shelf. 'Is it real?'

'A plaster cast,' said Misha. 'It was a horse. It died perfectly naturally. It's OK.'

'I like these,' said Ellen, moving towards a set of miniature shelves full of tiny bronze sculptures of eggs, every one of which was apparently trying to hatch out a different creature. 'But they're very, very strange.'

'I know,' said Misha. 'I like the baby dragon. And the boy who's half horse. I'm a bit like him, I think,' he said shyly, but Ellen had seen a new egg and could no longer hear him.

A single hole had been shattered in the shell and through it, a tiny, perfect hand stretched out, as though pleading for help. Ellen stopped breathing. She strained to see what was inside.

'Just a little wild child,' she whispered to herself. 'Crouching inside its egg, afraid.' Her eyes stung.

'But it wants someone to find it,' said Misha quickly. 'The right person.'

She looked up at him, startled, blinking away tears she hadn't known were falling.

'The egg doesn't look like the others either,' he pointed out. 'It's like an egg from another planet, or something. I don't think the child is meant to be from this world.'

But Ellen, overwhelmed with guilt and panic, could only see Lily.

Star child. Swan sister.

'I've got to go home,' she blurted, 'I've been out much too long. I've got to go.'

Misha walked back with her along the darkening lanes. They didn't talk much until they were standing right outside Midsummer House and then she said, 'It's Lily's birthday soon. She had a party last year. And it was rather – difficult. I don't think Mum will organise one this year.'

There was a great deal more she wanted to explain but that tiny bronze hand, forlornly signalling from inside its other-worldly egg had taken her words away.

'I'll come if you like,' said Misha at once. It was as if he didn't need Ellen to explain about Lily. As if he already understood everything he needed to know.

'Especially if there's food,' he added greedily. 'Food that isn't healthy food, I mean.'

'Would you come? Would you really?'

She was going to say more, about the christening and the swans' enchantment, about only being able to keep Lily for three years and a day, when Misha blurted out, 'And you needn't worry, Ellen. It's not your fault about your dad. You can't help what he did.'

'Whatever do you mean?' Ellen demanded. Unconsciously she clenched her fists. She couldn't believe what Misha had just said. 'What *has* he done? He hasn't done anything.' Her voice was shrill, breaking. She felt as if she was falling from a great height.

Misha flushed. 'You really don't know, do you?' he said. 'And I had to open my stupid mouth. Forget it, Ellen. I'm sorry. It doesn't matter.'

'It does matter,' she shouted. 'You tell me what he's supposed to have done if you're so clever!'

Misha looked away and mumbled, 'He was one of the team that helped to design the – that.' He gestured painfully towards the dark tower on the other side of the marsh, where the harsh lights were beginning to glitter against the country dusk.

'Granddad told me about it. I thought you knew. It's been going wrong for years. There was something leaking from the beginning but the company have only recently owned up now things are bad enough for ordinary people to notice; fish dying offshore, and seals . . . The last few years the swans on the marshes lost nearly all their cygnets. Mostly they don't hatch, or if they do, they're too weak or not properly – '

'*Don't!*' cried Ellen, to stop him. She covered her ears. 'Don't say it. Don't. It can't be my dad. He wouldn't do anything like that. I know he wouldn't. He's kind. He wouldn't hurt *anything* – '

And she turned and fled sobbing into the house.

7

Feathers in the Wind

'I didn't want to tell you,' said Cass painfully. She was pouring baby cereal into Lily's special bowl, stirring in soya milk. 'I hoped it would all be sorted out soon and you wouldn't have to know. Your father didn't want you to be upset.'

Ellen blew her nose. 'You should have told me. It was awful. Misha knowing and me – ' Her eyes started overflowing again.

'I'll make you a hot drink,' said Cass, helplessly.

'I don't want anything,' said Ellen, scrubbing at her face.

'It isn't really his fault,' said Cass. 'Your father was only one of the people who – '

'That doesn't make any difference,' said Ellen furiously. 'He shouldn't have had anything to do with it in the first place. It's killing everything. Like that old drowned city all over again. Can't you tell? The first day we came here I could *feel* it in the air, the sadness. As if the trees, the marshes, everything was trying to tell us something was wrong – '

'He has to earn a living,' Cass said. She was crushing a handful of tablets in a mortar. Since the doctor's visit, every evening, precisely as a laboratory experiment, she prepared Lily a high vitamin, high protein breakfast for the next day.

'He has to earn money somehow. We could never

have bought this house or even been able to afford to have another . . .' Her voice trailed away.

Ellen, unable to say another word, slowly shook her head, her eyes brimming.

She phoned Misha a few days later. 'I'm sorry I ran off like that,' she said. 'I suppose I just didn't want it to be true. You know you said you'd come to Lily's birthday party – did you really mean it? Will you still come? Even if – well, you know.'

'Sure,' said Misha. 'I'll come. We're temporary friends, remember. But are you OK? You sound peculiar.'

'No,' said Ellen. 'It's just that my father can't, er, manage to be here after all and last year – '

She could tell Misha was waiting for her to finish but she couldn't bring herself either to tell her fears for Lily aloud, or explain her vague hopes that Misha might help to keep her little sister safe. The magic of the swans was so dark and strange she was suddenly superstitiously terrified that she might strengthen it, even just by speaking of it. So she only said hastily, 'Oh, nothing. Come at about three tomorrow then. Cass promises she won't make one single healthy thing. And you needn't bother with a present or anything.'

But when Misha arrived he was carrying a small cardboard box that chimed faintly as he handed it to Ellen.

While Ellen opened the box, Lily hovered in the doorway, her eyes fixed somewhere above their heads, nervously sucking her fingers. She'd begun to suck them so often lately they had become chapped and sore. She was wearing a new flowery dress with a flouncy Victorian-style smock over it. Cass had recently trimmed her fringe so she looked more elfin than ever.

'Oh, Lily will love these,' Ellen exclaimed, pulling out a long string of bronze bells with a warm jangling sound. 'She likes anything that makes a beautiful sound.'

'I think they're actually meant to be cowbells,' said Misha, shedding two of his sweaters and unbuttoning his shirt collar. 'Each one has a different note.'

' – Star,' sang Lily, tiptoeing past them as if she'd never seen either of them in her life.

'These are for you, Lily-Lily,' said Ellen. 'So you can make your own star music.'

Cass came in and smiled tiredly when she saw the bronze bells. 'That's kind of you, Misha,' she said. 'I've put the tea things on the table, Ellen. Nothing healthy in sight as requested. Do you think you could help yourselves? For some reason I've got the most awful headache. What a silly day to get it, I'm cross with myself.'

'Go and lie down,' said Misha at once. 'That's what my mother does, and then it soon goes. Ellen and I could take Lily out for a walk, if that's OK,' he suggested. He sounded wistful, Ellen thought. As if he was quite keen to get back outside.

'You'd have to wrap her up really well, and be terribly careful with her,' said Cass doubtfully. But she looked relieved at the prospect of a quiet half hour to herself.

In a few minutes Misha and Ellen were walking along the lanes in a fine, cold mist, pushing Lily in her buggy. They'd had a hard time putting on her gloves and Lily's fingers still stuck out stiffly inside them, like scarecrow hands, as if they had nothing to do with her. And after a few minutes she'd managed to slip down inside her padded coat, so that her face was scarcely visible inside its enormous hood.

'It's absolutely sweltering in your house,' said Misha, taking a huge gulp of cold air. 'I know Granddad's mean with the heating. I actually get ice on the *inside* of my bedroom window. But your place is like a greenhouse. How do you bear it?'

'Mum always has it like that for Lily,' said Ellen. 'I don't notice now. But it is nice to be out. You push her buggy a minute. I want to do my coat up.'

'You know,' said Misha cautiously, fighting a smile. 'I don't want to be rude, but seeing her inside that big hood, with her fingers sticking out, your little sister really reminds me of E.T.'

Stung, Ellen opened her mouth to say Misha had absolutely no business making fun of Lily. She had the whole speech ready in a flash and it was so withering that after she'd made it she was going to snatch the buggy back from Misha and storm back home with Lily by herself and never talk to him again. She'd managed this long without friends. She could go on managing for ever if she had to.

Then she spoiled it entirely by laughing. She laughed until the tears poured down her face.

'Oh, Misha, she does!' she cried. 'I've never thought about it, but she really does!'

Suddenly it was a huge relief to talk about Lily's peculiarities with someone who accepted them so naturally. Misha didn't pretend he hadn't noticed anything. He didn't act super-polite the way other people did when they met Lily. Or say how *beautiful* she was, with that too nice, too sympathetic tone in their voices.

'And that funny thing she does with her fingers,' he said. 'As if she's signalling.'

'To other extra-terrestrials!' suggested Ellen, her eyes still streaming.

In the depths of her hood Lily gave a hoarse giggle, but when they peered quickly down, she was hanging over the side of her buggy, studying its wheels, her face demure.

'She understands, doesn't she?' said Misha, suddenly serious.

'Yes,' said Ellen, saying aloud for the first time what she had secretly thought for months. 'I think she does. In some ways she understands more than most people. She understands when people are telling the truth. What they're feeling. And she can't stand it if they pretend they're feeling something else. She starts to pinch herself or pull her own hair. She's like a truth machine, or I don't know, a Geiger counter or something. And there's something else –' Ellen glanced up from under her lids, to see if it was safe to go on. Misha waited.

'She understands the swans,' she said, scarcely audibly. 'They fly over our house and they call to her in their language and she understands.'

Ellen was watching Misha carefully as she was speaking and she noticed his expression didn't change so much as become fixed. It stayed so very much the same, it was as if he was turning into one of his grandfather's sculptures in front of her eyes. Then he gave a small, guarded smile and Ellen realised Misha was not going to tell her as she had hoped, that he too once understood the language of birds and animals. He doesn't want me to know about it, she thought sadly. He doesn't trust me enough. He's going to pretend he doesn't know what I'm talking about.

'It's freezing,' he said then. 'Let's run as far as the white fence to warm up. I'll race you with the buggy.'

Ellen, still battling with her disappointment, took a few seconds to hear what he had said.

Run? Race – with Lily's buggy? Ellen felt quite shaky with alarm. What would Cass say? Then suddenly she badly wanted to do it. Somewhere close by fear and sadness waited for her, like a heap of ugly old clothes she was forced to wear whether she wanted to or not. But for a few precious minutes, with this boy who was as freakish, maybe even as lonely as she was, she could be silly and almost ordinary.

'OK – On your marks. Ready, steady –' she shouted.

'Off go the charioteers!' yelled Misha, charging off.

Lily, who had been nodding dreamily inside her monk's hood, scarecrow fingers splayed, gave a startled whoop and hung on to the sides, her eyelids closing against the rush of cold wind.

Shrieking like banshees, with the buggy rattling drunkenly from one side of the lane to the other, Misha and Ellen tore through the mist to where the willows loomed over a shallow trickle of a stream behind a low white fence.

'Now it's your turn to be the charioteer,' commanded Misha, breathlessly. 'I think Lily's actually enjoying this, don't you?'

By the time they got back home all three children were flushed and dishevelled.

'Now remember, Lily,' murmured Misha, as they lifted the buggy back up the steps. 'You're on your honour not to say a single word.'

'That was nice,' said Ellen gratefully, when tea was over. 'Last year there were all these presents Lily didn't need or even notice, and all this party food she couldn't eat. It was like a bad dream. But today was fun. Very silly,' she added, grinning. 'But brilliant fun.'

Then as he was leaving, hauling his sweaters back over his head, she said shyly, 'Please don't be angry, but your granddad told me about – about how you used to understand what the birds said, and the animals . . . He said even going to school couldn't make you into an ordinary person and he was glad. That was why I told you about Lily and the swans.'

At first she thought Misha was going to stalk off in a huff. But instead he gave a sigh of immense relief.

'You don't think I'm mad then?' he said. 'I stopped telling anyone in the end. People got so weird about it. Mum took me to see a shrink and everything. I suppose it was hard for them, taking this little kid to the zoo for a nice treat and having to listen to him ranting about how miserable the animals were. I remember there was this bear – ' Misha fell silent, biting his lip remembering. 'The worst time was the dolphin pool at a safari park once. I could feel this terrible *scream* filling my head. As if they were begging me to do something –' He looked away quickly. 'I actually fainted. After that I tried to stop, er, understanding for a while. But then I felt terrible, hollow, like some kind of zombie. As if I was only half alive. And anyway I had this feeling that one day I was somehow going to need this weird thing. That it might turn out to be really important even if no one could understand much about it now. So I just make sure I stay away from dolphin pools.' He grinned shyly.

'I think I – ' Ellen stopped. She was still thinking how to say it. 'I don't understand animals the way you do, Misha,' she said slowly. 'But when we first came here I used to hear a kind of spooky voice. I don't know what it was or even where it was. It was sort of everywhere at once, and yet just inside my head at the same time.'

Misha was nodding. 'Everything's alive,' he said softly. 'Fire, stone, moss. That old copper beech tree there. Most people have to shut the aliveness out. They

72

try to forget. They've got too much else to think about. Work, money, wars.'

Ellen was thinking of her father, with his stereo turned up high.

'Lily can't shut it out ever,' she said, cold with understanding. 'She doesn't know how. Lily's like an open window that everything blows through. She has to listen to it *all*, the aliveness of everything. She has to see it all, all the time. What people are secretly thinking as well as what they say. How hurt the birds and animals are because of what – you know – humans do to them. It must be like having to watch all four TV channels at the same time, never being able to switch off the set. And tonight – ' She couldn't go on. Saying the words aloud seemed too dangerous when it came to it. As if she could conjure her terrors out of the air simply by naming them.

'Tonight?' Misha echoed. Under the thick brows, his brown eyes were almost almond shaped, she noticed, their expression sympathetic.

But Ellen lost her nerve completely.

'Well – you know, the swans might fly over calling again,' she said carelessly. 'And Lily gets so upset.'

'Well, I hope they don't come then,' he said quickly. But he looked away politely as he spoke, as if he didn't want Ellen to know he had caught her out in a lie.

I couldn't do it, she thought, after he had gone. I wanted to ask him to help me, but I just couldn't.

She had simply frozen, she thought, and her tongue had become paralysed even as it tried to form the words.

As if Ellen was enchanted too.

She went unhappily to her room, afraid even to think about the coming night and what it might bring. For now Misha had gone, the fears she had kept so

73

carefully at bay began to gather invisibly in the corners of her room like sticky cobwebs,

I won't even try to sleep, she told herself. It'll be much better if I don't. I'll read and I'll wait. I'll keep myself awake all night and then nothing can possibly happen.

But she had no idea what she was waiting for, what it was she dreaded so much that the print blurred before her eyes as she turned the pages so she could not have told anyone what she was reading.

She heard the clock strike one, then two. Her lids kept closing. Each time she caught herself and jumped guiltily, dragging herself awake, forcing herself back to her meaningless book.

She mustn't sleep. There was no one else to keep Lily safe.

So why hadn't she told Misha, who was the one person who would understand? The one other person who could help?

I felt ashamed, that's why, she thought. If we were a proper happy family, the swans couldn't have enchanted Lily. It's because something's gone wrong with us, it's all lopsided somehow at our house and I'm ashamed . . .

Her eyes shot open again. She had been dozing without knowing it.

'Please, Daddy,' she had been saying. 'Mum doesn't know I'm phoning you. But I really think you should be here tonight. Something terrible will happen if you don't.' But she couldn't hear his reply. His stereo was turned up too high and the opera singers drowned his sad, quiet voice.

Three o'clock struck.

Ellen's body was dissolving, floating.

Four. Four thirty.

I'm going to stay awake all night, she said to herself, pinching herself so hard she saw scarlet blotches behind her closed eyelids, the pain bringing her fiercely back into the room. *All night*.

A strong wind was getting up, blowing in from the sea. It was peaceful, lulling, lying in her warm bed listening to the gale howling around the house . . .

The sound of a banging door jarred her awake.

It'll wake Mum, she thought. Cass was probably still feeling ill. She had looked terrible last night.

Groggily Ellen stumbled from her room and across the landing in the colourless light of just before dawn.

It was Lily's door rhythmically slamming to and fro in the wind. Before she closed it, Ellen peeped in to make sure the sound hadn't frightened her little sister.

But a mess of white feathers littered the floor.

The curtains were blowing in the open window.

And Lily had gone.

8

A Maze of Water

Shock and confusion followed: phone calls, police cars racing up the drive of Midsummer House, their blue lights flashing, the house turned upside down, endless questions.

When she was no longer needed Ellen slid away to her room.

She had been trying to get someone to listen to her for years so she knew it was no use explaining to anyone now what had really happened. How she had followed the trail of feathers downstairs, to where the door to the garden stood open. How she had found the print of a tiny bare foot in the mud of a flowerbed. How the swans had borne Lily away at last to their wild marshy home.

And the mysterious voice once more beat in her head like wings.

Swan sister. Swan sister. Follow the signs. Follow the signs.

Ellen covered her ears. 'It's no use,' she wept. 'What's the use of saying that now? Lily's gone. I let them take her. I've tried to look after her so carefully ever since she was born, like the angel sister in the church, and they still took her. It's no use talking to me, whoever you are, I never understand anything you're trying to tell me. Why don't you go and tell Misha? He understands the –'

She sat up abruptly, scrubbing at her tears.

Follow the signs, repeated the voice.

Misha. How could Ellen have been so stupid?

She stole downstairs again. Through the open living-room door she saw Cass, painstakingly giving a description of Lily's appearance for the tenth time.

It broke Ellen's heart to see her mother's face so pinched and small. ' – a little white Viyella nightie down to her ankles,' she was repeating. 'And the cuffs were trimmed with lace . . .' Ellen could tell Cass was trying hard to stop her voice shaking. 'Her hair is fair, flyaway. I'd just cut her fringe . . .'

The police sergeant who had been scouting around by the back door came back inside shaking his head saying, 'It's impossible. No sign of anyone trying to break and enter. No tyre marks in the gravel. Just that one little footprint and then nothing – as if she simply vanished into thin air. When's the husband going to get here, does anyone know? If he's going to be much longer, I think someone should fetch Julie Lumkin to stop with this lady until he arrives. She shouldn't be left alone in this state.'

While the kind sergeant's back was turned, Ellen slipped out. She fled across the lawn and, climbing the fence, dropped awkwardly down into the meadow beyond. Ahead of her the countryside swept out towards the marshes. A thin mist hid the sea. Somewhere a ship hooted its warning and another answered it.

Follow the signs. Follow the signs.

How could she have been so stupid? What sort of signs had she been waiting for? Whacking great road signs saying 'Do this, Ellen!' 'Do that, Ellen!'

The signs had been under her nose all the time, woven so naturally into her everyday life she hadn't even noticed them.

Looking round quickly to make sure no one had seen her she set off at a run.

And Misha was already waiting by the stile in Dark Lane, chewing his nails.

'I know,' he said. 'They took her away. I heard them fly over from the marsh in the night. You knew yesterday, didn't you? That they might take her? Why ever didn't you tell me?'

'I couldn't,' said Ellen. 'I wanted to but – I suppose I've got used to trying to do it all myself. Only I can't. All the time the voice kept telling me to follow the signs and I couldn't even get that right. I wasn't looking for the right kind of signs. You were one, you see, but you were sort of too big to notice, somehow. So please, Misha, help me get her back. Apart from me, you're the only person who understands.'

'I want to help,' said Misha. 'Of course I do. But she could be anywhere out there.' He was half talking to himself. 'Really we need a boat. I wonder if Mary –'

'Do you mean Marsh Mary?' cried Ellen. 'Do you know her, then.'

More signs I've been missing, she thought, dismayed, remembering how she had been drawn to Mary the day Cass had taken her to St Aidan's church, and how the woman had burst in, right in the middle of Lily's christening. Then Ellen had bought that book in Aldeburgh . . . I'm so *stupid*, she thought.

'Yes,' said Misha in surprise. 'I've known her for ages. She's got a couple of old dinghies. I wonder if she'd let us borrow one – The marshes are really made up of hundreds of little islands, you see. If we rowed around a bit we might get some clue where she is –'

'Oh, Misha!' Overwhelmed, Ellen was suddenly

weeping with great tearing sobs. 'I keep picturing Lily. She must be so cold and frightened. So lonely. I can't *bear* it.' She covered her face, her shoulders shaking.

Misha looked as if he was going to say something but thought better of it, patting her awkwardly on the back instead.

'You'd better go home now,' he said gently. 'Or they'll think you've gone missing too. I'll slip down to Mary's place and if we can borrow the boat, I'll fetch you before it's light tomorrow. Then you can get out and back without anyone missing you.'

But Ellen had gripped him by the sleeve. 'You think Lily *wanted* to go with the swans, don't you?' she said urgently.

'I don't know, Ellen,' said Misha. His brown almond eyes gazed steadily back at her. 'This whole thing is so strange. It feels almost familiar, somehow. Like remembering a dream. I think you're being much too hard on yourself. This was going to happen whatever you did. As if it *had* to happen. Like – I don't know – Fate or something. That day I saw you and Lily at Aldeburgh I already knew . . . I can't explain exactly. Only I don't know why.'

When Ellen tried to sneak back in through her own back door, she collided with a furious Mrs Lumkin.

'Now wherever have you been, you naughty girl,' scolded the woman. 'I've been at my wits' end. I've just put your mum to bed. The doctor's given her something to help her sleep. I don't know when your dad will get here so you'd better come home with me. You can have little Simeon's bed. I'll put him in with Samuel for tonight.'

'I'd rather stay here with Mum, honestly,' said Ellen swiftly. She was speaking the truth. But she had also once seen little Simeon from a distance, plastered in mud, spitting at passing cars. 'She might need something. I know Daddy won't be long.'

In fact her father arrived not long after, but although Ellen had been watching the clock, longing for the moment when she heard his car, and the sound of his key in the lock, she knew as soon as she saw him that he could help neither her nor Lily. He hardly even seemed to see Ellen properly.

'Where's Cass?' he said at once. 'She hasn't left you on your own?'

'She's asleep,' said Ellen. 'The doctor –'

'I'll go up to her,' he said. 'She can't just collapse every time there's a crisis. She has to learn to face reality some time.' He rushed past her without another word.

Ellen's legs gave way suddenly and she sat down numbly right where she was at the foot of the stairs. Is that what he's been thinking all this time, she thought. He never said, before. There was a far-off ache in her throat that seemed to belong to someone else.

A small blue butterfly, woken from hibernation, was fluttering bewildered against the window.

It'll die, Ellen thought dully, but there's nothing I can do about it. And she went on sitting where she was, listening to the subdued voices of her parents upstairs, while the butterfly went on beating its tiny body against the glass, trying to get out.

All night Ellen was rowing along the misty waterways amongst the islands of the marsh, searching for Lily. Sometimes she heard her singing, but the mist was always too thick or the channels too narrow for the boat to go any further. It was a relief to wake to the real-life sound of Misha's stones raining against her window. She threw on her clothes and ran down to find him waiting for her.

'Mary remembers you,' he said. 'From the christening. She remembers the swans flying over too. You won't have to explain to her. I know most people think she's nuts but she understands things other people don't.'

'Can we borrow the boat?'

Misha nodded. 'But we'll have to hurry. It'd be better if you had a bike, really. I cycled up here.'

'I've got a bike,' said Ellen. 'But I've only just learned to ride it. You mustn't mind if I wobble.'

They sped down the lanes in the muted light that comes before true dawn and Ellen's wobbles were under control by the time they reached the other side of the forest.

Marsh Mary's house was an extraordinary cross between a wooden cabin and an upturned boat, beached on a high patch of sandy ground, between the watery marshes and the sea. Smoke rose from a tin chimney in erratic spirals. Mary herself was sitting outside on her front step, absently petting the ears of a gangling setter puppy, her hair wound into a flowery scarf. Despite the cold, her feet were bare and her toenails, Ellen was astonished to notice, were painted bright scarlet.

'Come in,' she said. 'The kettle's on. You can have toast too, if you want it.'

'We haven't got time,' said Ellen. 'I mean, thank you. But we mustn't. My little sister – '

'Haven't you ever heard of Romulus and Remus, girl?' said Marsh Mary sharply.

'Ye-es,' said Ellen, deciding Marsh Mary was madder than she had thought. 'They were twin babies. The wolves brought them up. And then they founded

Rome. I think,' she added uncertainly. 'The children, not the wolves.'

'Well, there you are,' said Mary unhelpfully. 'And I'll tell you your sister is perfectly safe where she is, among the swans. Probably safer than she's been since the day she was born.'

'That's a stupid thing to say,' cried Ellen angrily. 'She was only wearing a little nightie. She'll freeze. And there's nothing for her to eat. She's not a frog. She can't eat worms and beetles. She needs vitamins – I thought you'd understand. I thought you were going to help us get her back.'

Marsh Mary pursed her lips. 'I never said that,' she said. 'I just told that boy there I'd lend you my boat so you can look for her. Which I will. But what will happen if you find her I don't know. It isn't up to me, I'm afraid. And it isn't up to you either, Ellen. This is a bigger story than yours or mine.'

She rose to her feet and went into the shack. Misha stayed on the step, stroking the puppy.

'Her tea is absolute poison,' he warned in a low voice. 'But her coffee's worse. They're both very black. The toast will probably be OK.'

Reluctantly Ellen followed the woman into the cabin where a copper kettle had begun to sing over a polished black stove.

'This is kind of you but I have to get back before they notice I'm missing,' she said worriedly. She was faintly startled by the inside of Marsh Mary's home which was unexpectedly full of beautiful things. Wooden shelves carved with fruit and flowers. Delicate china. Bright rugs.

Marsh Mary ignored her and went on pouring a stream of boiling water into an apple-green teapot.

'Are you a fighter, Ellen?' she demanded suddenly.

Ellen jumped at the abruptness of the question, then jumped again, finding herself staring into the unfriendly eyes of a large gull which was perching on the back of a graceful lyre-backed chair.

'Don't mind Boris. The last oil slick nearly did for him but I pulled him through. He's happy enough to have a quiet life these days. You didn't answer me, girl. I asked if you were a fighter?'

'I – Yes,' said Ellen, reaching a decision which surprised her. 'Yes I am.'

'You'll need to be,' remarked Mary tersely. 'How many sugars?'

Ellen took the thin white cup, looking nervously at the scalding black fluid it contained. 'Do you still write stories?' she asked politely. 'I bought one of your books in Aldeburgh.'

Marsh Mary clattered crockery on her dresser. Her mouth was set in a straight line, but her hand trembled, Ellen saw.

'No I don't,' she said. 'And I daresay you're like all those other know-alls that won't leave a person in peace, and you'll pester away at me until you know the reason why, won't you? So I'll tell you and then let that be the end of it. It's because there comes a time, Ellen Carson, when all the stories have been told and all the words spoken and the world is still in one hell of a mess and you realise you haven't done it one bit of good.'

'I offended her,' said Ellen later, as Misha untied the dinghy, handed Ellen down beside him and began to row out into the water.

'She hates talking about her writing,' said Misha. 'She might have been worse. I think she actually likes you.'

Within minutes Ellen and Misha were gliding

through a watery maze, heading into the hidden heart of the marshes.

In some places the channels were barely wide enough for the oars. In others a skim of ice crackled and sank as the boat forged onwards. Misha rowed steadily, peering through the faint mist at the reedy, colourless tussocks which were the islands.

'They look better in summer,' he said, sensing Ellen's disappointment. 'When the sea lavender's flowering and the other wild flowers are out. There are even orchids. Bird watchers come here, you know. The RSPB have built hides for them. This is only part of an enormous bird sanctuary.'

'It's awfully strange,' whispered Ellen. 'Like another world. Another time.'

Somewhere in the marsh a bird gave a metallic shriek.

'What did it say?' Ellen demanded quickly.

But Misha shook his head. 'It isn't like that,' he said. 'I can't use it to spy on things. They have to *want* me to know.'

'Then we might never get Lily back, if the swans want to hide her from us.' Ellen's throat closed with sorrow. She couldn't say another word.

'No, we might not,' said Misha. '*If* that's what they want,' he added strangely.

They rowed in silence after that. Some islands had stunted trees or overhanging bushes growing on them. Sometimes the boat startled dull brown birds invisible amongst dull brown grasses, until they went whirring up into the sky uttering cries of alarm. But otherwise each reedy mount seemed as colourless and featureless as the others to Ellen.

After a while she fell into a kind of trance. She stopped worrying about whether they had stayed out too long or if they might lose their way. It was as if there was nothing in the world except the marsh and its windswept islands, the boat and the oars rhythmically dipping in and out of the ice-skimmed water.

Lily, Lily, she thought. If you're really here, try to tell me, somehow.

Suddenly she was alert with every cell of her body.

'This island, Misha,' she shouted excitedly. 'The one with the thorn bush. Can we stop? Can I get out?'

'Maybe,' he said dubiously, shipping the oars. 'You might sink, though. What have you seen?'

'Nothing,' she said. 'Nothing I can explain.'

Follow the signs. Follow the signs.

A stunted thorn bush, a white feather on the wind, a flash of faded blue, the colour of the butterfly she had pitied, the day Lily disappeared . . .

Maybe none of these meant anything at all. Yet Ellen's every sense was shouting out.

Misha steadied her as she clambered out. She stepped cautiously on to wiry, innocent-looking grass. As soon as she trusted her weight, oily black mud squelched upwards, sucking at her wellingtons. But she'd already snatched something from the thorns.

'I'm sinking, Misha. Help me get my wellies unstuck,' she panted.

'I've got you,' said Misha, grabbing her around the waist and hauling her back into the dinghy so that the boat rocked violently.

Ellen's eyes were bright. Her cheeks flushed.

'She's been here,' she said, triumphantly flopping back into her place. 'Look.'

She was clutching a scrap of white cloth. 'It's from Lily's nightie. She was here. We're going to find her, I can feel it. I know we will, she's so close.'

85

'It's time to go back now, though,' said Misha firmly. 'Or they'll miss you.'

'I don't care about that,' cried Ellen. 'That won't matter a bit, if we find Lily, will it? I can explain to them. Misha, she's been out here for a whole night as it is. The longer we leave her –'

'Ellen,' interrupted Misha. There was an edge to his voice she had never heard before. 'Listen! Really listen properly. And tell me what you hear, what you feel.'

Ellen closed her eyes sullenly, unwillingly concentrating on the sounds around her. She could hear the wind in the reeds, water lapping round the boat, the occasional peep of a moorhen, the cries of gulls.

'I can't hear anything,' she was going to say crossly. 'Nothing at all.'

And then she did.

It was not so much a sound, as a feeling, as if part of her was flowing out into the marsh, and the marsh was sending her in return its messengers of rush, thorn, butterfly.

It's like the day we drove through the forest and found the house, she thought. Everything was so alive, so sad. Talking to me. Trying to tell me something was wrong.

And somewhere in the heart of the islands she could feel Lily, but a new Lily, one she had never known. Not a frightened indoor Lily buttoned up in frilly smocks and tights and put to bed at the same time each night in her silvery moonlit grove.

It was hard to get a clear sense of who or what Lily was now, because of the great wings, the downy breasts, the hissing, snake-like necks that surrounded her, protected her, but one thing was clear. Marsh Mary was right.

For the first time in her life Lily was happy.
And she didn't want to come home.

9

Swan Child

When Ellen let herself back into Midsummer House the curtains were drawn and there was still no sound or movement from upstairs. 'I'm not going to give up,' she said fiercely. 'I'm never going to give up until we've got Lily back. She's my sister. My human sister. She *can't* stay out on the marsh for the rest of her life!'

But she was bitterly hurt. Despite the troubles of the last three years, Ellen had tried to be the most loving sister Lily could have. Like the angel at St Aidan's, towing her sister bravely along under the stars.

Now Midsummer House felt so large and lonely, so *wrong* without Lily tiptoeing through its rooms, crooning to herself.

'Oh, I miss her so much,' she whispered.

But Lily felt safer amongst the mud and reeds, beyond the reach of humans, encircled by heavy white wings, fierce hissing necks. Lily was happy now. And Lily hadn't been truly happy since the day of the christening, Ellen thought. Since that day she had been haunted; lost. All these years Ellen had been desperately trying to protect her, when all the time Lily had been yearning for her swan family. It didn't make sense. It was as if one of the brothers in the story had torn off his nettle shirt, saying, 'Take it back! I'd rather be a swan.'

It's because the swans enchanted her, she thought

angrily. They've *made* Lily forget us. They're angry with Dad because of what he did. That's why they took Lily, to punish him. They think it's his fault their babies are dying . . .

And maybe it is, she thought, though she longed with all her heart not to believe it. Maybe they're right. But it wasn't my fault. And I love Lily. I want her to be my sister for always.

Her father came downstairs at last, his face yellow with tiredness, deep shadows under his eyes.

'Your mother's still asleep,' he said. 'God knows what was in the tablets that doctor gave her. I'm going into Ipswich to see what the police think they're up to. They should be organising a major search. A tiny girl disappears from her cot in the middle of the night and no one *does* anything. It's ridiculous. Where the hell does Cass keep the muesli now? She never keeps anything in the same place two days running.'

Ellen got the cereal out of the cupboard for him and lifted two bowls down from the shelf. As she opened the refrigerator she yawned hugely. After her morning out on the marshes, she felt as if she'd been up for several days already. 'I was supposed to go back to school today,' she remembered. 'But it's too late. Do I have to go?'

To her surprise her father didn't insist. 'Stay with your mother for today,' he said. 'She's still very shocked.'

'Aren't you cross with her any more, then?' asked Ellen.

Her father put down his spoon. 'Cross? I wasn't cross. I was just so – When the police phoned me . . . I felt so helpless. I suppose I just wanted someone to be angry with.'

'You didn't want to come to live here, did you,

Daddy?' said Ellen. 'But you let Mum buy the house anyway. Was it because of the power station you didn't want to come?'

She was watching her father closely. She saw how he flinched away, then tried to smile to cover his discomfort.

'No,' he said at last. And then he said awkwardly, 'Well, in a way, I suppose. Perhaps. That might have been one reason.'

He got up from the table and began to refasten his tie more tightly.

'You see, I have to live in the real world, Ellen,' he said. 'I have to survive. I have to look after you all. When you're grown up you'll find out what it's like. For now, just be glad your mother and I protect you. The world is a cruel place, you know.'

But remembering her little sister nestling contentedly amongst wild swans, Ellen didn't believe him. Her father was always saying that the world was cruel, that nature was harsh. It gave him the excuse to do what he liked, she thought. No matter what harm it did.

'The world isn't cruel,' she said, astonishing herself. 'But it's truthful,' she whispered, seeing her father was no longer listening. 'It can't bear us to tell lies, that's the trouble.'

Soon Ellen's life had fallen into a new pattern. Each morning before it was light she and Misha rowed out amongst the islands, searching, calling. And each morning she was back before her mother was awake. Ellen's father was back in London now and Cass slept late these days. Even when she was up and dressed she seemed scarcely aware of Ellen, hardly speaking to her unless it was necessary. Perhaps there were no words large enough for the horror Cass was living through.

Ellen was watchful of her mother, her heart aching for her, but she kept a careful distance as if showing her love would only harm Cass more. Once or twice, yearning to reach out to her and knowing no other way, Ellen picked wild flowers from the hedgerow, leaving them on the kitchen table for Cass to find. But her mother never seemed to see them, and each time Ellen came home to a handful of wilting weeds. At school her hours passed in a daze and she remembered nothing of what she did there.

The only part of her life that was real to Ellen these days was the time she spent on the marshes.

One morning the sky was leaden with coming snow. Mary told them not to take the boat out, but Ellen refused to give in. 'You asked me if I was a fighter and I am. We're still going.'

The sky was so overcast Misha had to hold up a storm lantern to light their way, while Ellen, who rowed as well as Misha now, sculled along, coaxing the dinghy through broken ice that bobbed on the dark peaty water, like marshmallows in chocolate.

Long before they stumbled back on to land, teeth chattering, the boat was white, the air swarming with dry white grains that burned where they touched the skin. But still the children called and searched until the usual time.

Misha never once told her that it was hopeless, that they would never find Lily if the swans chose to hide her so well, nor did Ellen speak about her fears that Lily might be dead of cold, hunger, drowning. Instead they went calling along the marsh, day after day, week after week and soon Ellen could hardly remember that her life had been spent in any other way.

Until the mornings became lighter, the dun-coloured

islands grew greener and the air warmer and one day Ellen rested her oars, took off her specs, tugged her sweater over her head, and said, fanning herself, 'Misha, it's nearly spring, you know.' And they listened in astonishment to the raucous birdsong all around them.

Then they heard it. The small pure voice.

'Row, row, row the boat, gently down the stream . . .'

'That's Lily,' cried Ellen, the colour draining from her face. 'I used to sing that to her, when she was sad. When she was tiny. But I never heard her sing it.'

' . . . life is but a dream,' the voice continued. Then the singer burst out laughing, a bird's rapid outpouring of sound; liquid, careless.

'It's coming from over there,' said Misha urgently. 'Pull to the left a bit more, and head for those overhanging brambles – Blast! We can't get through, they're too thick. We'd be slashed to ribbons if we try.'

'But she's so close,' pleaded Ellen.

'Row, row, row the boat . . .' the voice crooned. She sounded so near Ellen felt sure she could plunge her hand amongst the thorns and catch hold of Lily's small, transparent hand. ' . . .gently down the stream . . .'

'She's teasing us,' said Ellen. 'Misha, she *knows* we're here – Lily!' she shouted. 'Lily, it's me, Ellen!'

The singing stopped abruptly. In the sudden silence, the whole marsh seemed to be listening; every root, leaf, stem and particle of earth connected, living, aware.

'Lily,' called Ellen standing up in the boat, rocking it dangerously. 'Can you hear us? Please come home. We miss you so badly. Mummy's so worried. She's ill. She can't eat or sleep. And –'

A white shape reared out of the water with a hiss

like a cobra, sending Ellen staggering back into her seat. Suddenly the boat was surrounded, the air filled with harsh protesting voices . . .

And from its thorny hiding place, a small voice cried on one note, already fading like the sorrowful call of a marsh bird. *'Not yet. Not yet. Not yet.'*

'The swans told you something,' Ellen accused Misha, as they tied up Mary's boat and headed for their bikes. 'You needn't pretend. You get a funny expression on your face when you're listening like that. You knew Lily was safe, didn't you? You knew she mightn't want to come home with us too. And now you know something else.'

Misha was fiddling with the valve on his back tyre. 'The swans think you don't understand why they took Lily,' he said hesitantly. 'They didn't do it to punish anyone, or to replace their lost children. They want Lily because she's – because she understands things other people don't.'

'You mean, like you and Marsh Mary? But that's crazy, she's just a little girl – '

'She's more special than me or Mary. It's not easy to explain, but *different* children, children like Lily, are born into the world more often now. They might seem odd to some people, and sometimes they seem to bring a lot of pain and sadness with them at first, but that's because they've come to teach us . . .' He faltered.

'Teach us what?' demanded Ellen.

'How to live together, how to look after the earth,' he said unhappily. 'To put right the harm that's been done. And I hate saying this,' Misha burst out. 'I know you must feel awful about your dad.'

'And the swans *knew* all the time that we were going to come to live at Midsummer House? That Lily was going to be born there?'

Ellen was horrified. Yet she also knew it was true. She had known it without properly understanding, from her very first day in Suffolk.

'Yes,' he said. 'They want her to learn their ways. To live among wild things.'

'But she's a person,' said Ellen, shaking her head. 'You're wrong about her, Misha. She's just a little girl who – she couldn't even *feed* herself when she left. Mum always had to feed her.'

Without Ellen noticing, Marsh Mary had come up behind them.

'Go home, Ellen,' she said calmly. 'It might be better if you didn't come again for a while. You know Lily's safe. Leave her where she is. She has her own reasons for being there. She's happy, you heard for yourself. She was a freak, an oddity in your world. She was lost and heartbroken. The marsh is her proper home now.'

'No it isn't,' shouted Ellen. 'Her home is with us, my mum and dad and me. We might not be the most perfect family in the world but we're her own human family and we love her. I know you can't understand,' she blazed at Mary. 'You love animals so much, you don't think humans count at all. You think all humans do is ruin everything. *That's* why you stopped writing books. I'm going back home to tell my mother and I'm going to bring her down here to find my sister and you can't stop me.'

Mary looked sad. 'Of course,' she said quietly. 'You must tell her, Ellen. You can even borrow my dinghy if you need it. But I'm afraid it won't do either of you any good.'

In the end Ellen had no choice about telling Cass. When she got back home her mother was already up, pacing the kitchen in her dressing gown.

'Perhaps you'd like to tell me where you've been,' she said, swallowing tiny tablets with the help of a glass of water. 'Have you any idea how I felt when I found you'd gone? Have you *any* idea?'

'I'm sorry,' said Ellen. 'I didn't mean to worry you. But if you'd only let me tell you –'

'Go on then,' said Cass tiredly, sitting down abruptly as if her legs had suddenly given way. 'And this had better be extremely good.'

These last months Cass had lost weight. Her towelling robe almost drowned her now and her wrist and ankles had become so thin Ellen found it hard to look at them. Cass looked too much like Lily. Even the blurred pain in her eyes, the bewildered, questioning expression was Lily's.

'I've been looking for Lily,' explained Ellen. 'Every morning I've been out on the marsh in a dinghy, with Misha. I can row now. Misha showed me how. And I've been calling and looking. And today – ' She swallowed.

'Go on.' Cass's expression wasn't encouraging.

'We *heard* her. Singing,' Ellen added. 'On a little island, but we couldn't see her, because it was too thorny to get close, and we didn't have anything to cut the brambles with. She's with the swans,' Ellen repeated, feeling increasingly uncertain as Cass went on staring at her. 'And I can take you, if you like. Marsh Mary says we can borrow her boat.'

'Are you telling me you've been wandering around the countryside for *months*, risking your life in that crazy old tramp's leaky boat?' Cass was breathing quickly now, her knuckles whitening.

'She's not a tramp,' said Ellen bravely. 'She was a writer but she stopped because all the stories had already been told. And the boat isn't leaky. Oh, Mum, please come. Let me take you. I know where Lily is. Honestly. Believe me. Have I ever, ever once told you a single lie?'

Cass tugged her hands through her uncombed hair and suddenly closed her eyes. A tear seeped slowly under her right eyelid. 'No,' she said at last, dashing other tears away, opening her eyes again. 'To be fair, you haven't. Not that I know of, anyway, and never over anything important. And I can see you believe you're telling the truth. But it's impossible, Nell. What you're saying belongs to the world of fairy tales and your father's right, I have to face reality now. It's been too long. There's no chance Lily could have survived this long. I'd do anything to have my little girl back,' her voice broke and she swallowed hard. 'But I can't bear, Ellen sweetheart, to come out with you on a wild-goose chase, or swan chase or any kind of chase. I just can't *bear* it . . .' She covered her face, rocking slightly in her chair. 'I'm sorry, Ellen. I know you loved Lily too. I know I'm an awful mother to you just now. Just be patient with me. I'll be all right again soon.'

'Mum,' implored Ellen, seizing her mother's thin arm, gently forcing Cass to look at her. 'Please. Just come this once. I'll never ask you again. Please. Look at me.'

'Oh, Nell,' Cass said, almost laughing now, through her tears. 'Those eyes of yours. When you turn them on me like that, what chance do I have? I must be mad even to think of it, but I'll come . . .'

Cass knew how to row too, Ellen discovered to her surprise. They took an oar each and the boat sped rapidly forward with each strong pull. For the first few minutes Ellen's mother looked around her almost contentedly, as if she was on holiday, pointing out the wild flowers growing everywhere; violets matted amongst the roots of bushes, lady's smock, crowsfoot and once a single clump of cowslips nodding on a grassy mound.

'I was taught wild-flower names at my village school,' she said proudly. 'I can't have been more than six or seven, because my parents died soon after and I had to move away. But I've never forgotten them. I used to recite the names to myself before I went to sleep. Like a kind of magic. As if naming them would somehow bring them back to me – or bring me back to them . . .' She fell silent again and Ellen knew her mother was thinking of Lily now.

It seemed odd, seeing Cass out in the sunlight and open air. Lately Ellen almost only ever saw Cass indoors, making herself endless cups of coffee or curled up in her chair, the curtains drawn, staring silently into space. Out of doors her pinched, white face looked curiously exposed. She was shivering, obviously feeling the cold even with her jacket buttoned up to the chin. The heating was still kept turned up high at Midsummer House as if Cass needed that tropical warmth herself now, to survive.

As they rowed deeper into the watery maze of tiny islands, Cass kept commenting, trying to laugh, 'I must be mad, mustn't I, letting you persuade me to come out in this thing. What would your father say?'

And then she'd ask anxiously, 'And you're sure we're going in the right direction?'

Each time Ellen said breezily, 'Oh yes. I know we are. You'll hear her voice in a moment, then you'll know I'm telling the truth.'

But as time went on Ellen felt less confident in her powers of navigation. She was convinced that they were in the right place, only large quantities of mud seemed to have been dislodged mysteriously from the banks since the early morning, clogging the channels, making them even narrower. Several times Ellen and her mother had to use the oars to push the boat away from the islands. Their progress grew painfully slow. It was heavy work. Cass, no longer strong, soon seemed tired and discouraged.

'Sorry. It honestly wasn't like this before, Mum,' admitted Ellen after a while. 'I don't understand it at all.'

To make things worse, an odour of something rank and rotting began to fill the air. This morning, with Misha, the dawn marsh had been a wild enchanted land, Ellen thought, bewildered. Perhaps she was seeing more truly by the strong midday sunlight, but the sight made her feel ill. A coffee-coloured froth slopped greasily at the water's edge and for the first time she noticed a lurid green waterweed growing so thickly it turned the water around the boat into a sullen soup, choking up the channels, making it even harder to row. The tangled mat of weed, like a grotesque fishing net, had trapped all kinds of junk: discoloured lumps of polystyrene, rusting bedsprings, old fertilizer sacks, soft-drink cans. Why had she never noticed that human beings were steadily turning the marshes into a watery rubbish dump?

What have we done? she thought. *What have we done?* And she remembered Misha telling her about the dolphins and the silent scream that had filled his head.

Cass was plainly exhausted now so Ellen took over both oars. It took every scrap of courage and willpower she possessed to keep battling through the evil-smelling water, as if the stink was not just a stink, but a deadly despair, breathing up out of the marsh like a poisonous gas. 'I *think* that's the island,' she said, doubtfully. The smell made it almost impossible to think. 'It's brambly like the swan island was. But don't worry, I've brought some cutters this time.'

She reached out of the boat, trying to hack at the overhanging brambles. But either they were a species of super-bramble or the cutters were blunt, because she couldn't make any impression on the fleshy stems. Instead the cutters skidded off, sinking their sappy blades into her fingers.

'Ow,' she said dropping them back into the boat, sucking her hand in dismay.

Cass, looking queasy, was shivering in the midday heat. 'This is a mistake, Nell,' she said. 'You've tried your best, now let's go back home. I've got an awful headache. I really don't feel well at all.'

'No,' said Ellen stubbornly. 'Lily was *here*. She was singing "Row the Boat". If we sing back to her she'll answer us, I know she will.'

'No, Nell, I really don't want – '

'Come on,' insisted Ellen. 'We can't give up now.' Fiercely, she began to sing.

After a while, at a distance, a small voice very lightly, dreamily joined with hers.

Ellen's heart leapt. Now Cass would have to see. Now everything would come right.

So why was Cass pulling her jacket more closely around her, her hand to her nose, trying to block out the stench of the polluted water? Why were her eyes blankly staring into nothing?

Ellen stopped singing, faltering, bewildered.

The small voice carried on alone.

'. . . life is but a dream . . .'

'You *see*!' cried Ellen triumphantly. 'Lily *is* here. We've just got to cut through these brambles.' With new energy she began to saw at the massive stems, heedless of thorns.

Cass shook her head exhaustedly. 'What are you saying, Nell? You're just imagining things. I heard you singing, that's all. No one else.'

'But you heard her,' protested Ellen, distressed. 'Lily was singing back to me. There were two of us singing. You *must* have heard. *Call* her, Mum. Call her and she'll answer you.'

'Don't,' cried Cass, burying her face. 'Don't keep on with this awful game, Ellen. Let's go home now. I know you want to help but I can't bear this – '

'Mum, *call* her. She'll answer you – OK, I'll call her for you. Lily! Lily! Mummy's here. She's come to find you. She wants to hear your voice.'

Again the whole marsh was hushed, listening. The only sound was Cass, desperately trying to muffle her sobs.

Then a small questioning voice.

'Mummy?'

'Listen!' Ellen hissed, relentlessly pulling Cass's hands away from her face. 'She's *answering* you. Can't you hear her? She's talking. She's not just singing the way she used to. She's really talking. She said 'Mummy". Call her name, Mum. Tell her you want to bring her back home.'

But Cass, uncontrollably weeping now, seized both oars and began to row with frantic speed away from the island of the swans.

'You couldn't hear her,' said Ellen appalled. 'She spoke but you couldn't hear, could you?'

She twisted herself round desperately to look back the way they had come. Behind its barrier of thorns, as though enchanted, the island of the swans was already blurring into invisibility. But for one moment against

100

the shadowy reeds Ellen saw a small white figure gazing after them; a child so enfolded by arching necks, sheltering wings, that she herself seemed winged, part swan. Ellen rubbed her eyes, doubting what she'd seen. But in her head the small voice repeated, questioningly, 'Mummy? Mummy?'

And again that mournful cry on one note, fading, as the boat left the island far behind. 'Not yet. Not yet. Not yet.'

10

Midsummer's Eve

Ellen didn't go out in the boat with Misha again. In fact, by some silent common consent, they ceased to see each other at all. She had failed to convince Cass. She had failed to find Lily. And now it was far too painful to face her friend. For Ellen believed she had failed only because something was terribly wrong with her family, and she was ashamed.

She could bear school because it was easy enough for her to fade into the background now. No one at school either knew her or cared much about her. Even the name-calling of the other children was more out of habit now than malice. But Misha knew what Ellen was thinking, he understood what she felt almost as soon as she did, and if she was with him she'd see again that ready sympathy in his dark, almond-shaped eyes. She would have to think again, feel again and decide what to do about Lily. When all she wanted now was to hide herself away with her ugly hurt, like an injured bird.

She began to spend hours reading, either in her room or in private corners of the house. The rest of the time she wandered the countryside in a daze.

Someone or something had trusted her to help, to put things right, and she had not done it.

Every single thing reminded her of her failure. The chemical scum floating in the streams. The disease-stricken trees between Midsummer House and the marsh. The orange flares harshly illuminating the tower at night. The oil she brought home on her shoes from her solitary walks along the shore. Even the cry of the wild birds flying over the marshes through veils of summer rain.

And closest of all, the small empty room across the landing from Ellen's own. Sometimes Ellen would discover herself daydreaming in Lily's room without remembering how she had got there, or even why she had come; she would just find herself sitting on the floor, fingering one of those tiny flowery dresses, or staring out of the window, lost in memories of a baby girl who had once laughed and cried like other baby sisters.

And it felt then as if part of Ellen, too, was lost forever, as if her life would never again have its old, bright colours, and scents. As if all the magic had fled from it, leaving behind only the grey husks of habit.

The last time she'd tried to telephone her father she got the answer phone; his voice tired, fading in and out as though he was talking across oceans. Remembering Misha joking sadly about underwater conversations, she softly replaced the receiver and didn't ring again.

The truth was that they were not a proper family any more. Only Ellen and Cass, living quietly in the same house, meeting over their silent meals of tinned ravioli or frozen chicken pie, always kind to each other, rarely meeting each other's eyes. Separate, solitary, too numb to be sad.

Then, one afternoon in early summer, Ellen came home to find the kitchen door standing wide open and muddy bootprints tracking across the kitchen floor. Cass wasn't in her usual chair, curled up, staring into space. In fact she was nowhere to be seen.

In a panic Ellen rushed out into the garden where, to her astonishment, she found her mother in a filthy T-shirt and ancient pair of jeans, fiercely rooting up weeds, mud streaking her thin white arms and forehead.

'This garden,' said Cass breathlessly, without slackening her grip on the bleached tubers of a gigantic dandelion, 'is completely out of control. It practically shrieked at me to come out here and restore order. If you want any tea, Nell, there's a couple of egg sandwiches under the stripy cloth.'

The root came out with a rush. With an expression of satisfaction Cass slung it into the wheelbarrow with the rest of the mounting pile. 'I'm not hungry,' said Ellen. 'I'll help you do that if you like.'

It was a shock to see Cass so energetic after all these months. Ellen wasn't sure whether to be pleased or alarmed.

'No thanks,' said Cass, to Ellen's surprise. 'I think I need to do it by myself. It seems to be clearing my head.'

So for the next few days Ellen watched through windows, doorways, or from the fields beyond, looking back at the house from a safe distance, as her mother stubbornly mowed, clipped, dug and raked, hauled out thistly armfuls of weeds and burned smoky, evil-smelling pyres of green stuff.

Until gradually the shape of the garden re-emerged from the dishevelled meadow it had become, and with the reappearance of the garden came something else, something less visible, but every bit as real.

Slowly Cass herself began to come back to life.

'It's so beautiful out here, Nell,' Cass called to her, one afternoon, tying up toppling spires of rosy mallow with garden twine. 'I can't think why I haven't spent more time in it. I keep uncovering fruit bushes. There's practically an entire orchard under all this outrageous honeysuckle. There's an old strawberry bed by the wall, if we can manage to keep the slugs off it, and I've found some raspberry canes, look! If I stake them we'll have loads of berries in a month or two.'

That evening Cass made soup for supper and Ellen companionably helped to scrub and slice the vegetables. It was a simple enough meal, and the first real cooking Cass had done since Lily vanished.

While the pot simmered, Cass had a hot bath to sluice off the mud and Ellen grated lemon, then chopped the chives and parsley Cass had discovered under the weeds. As she chopped she heard Cass humming along to the radio upstairs.

Nowadays the two of them usually ate their meals scrunched up one end of the giant dining table, like guilty refugees who had no right to be there, but today, when Cass came downstairs again, smelling of scented bath oil, she insisted on spreading a pretty cloth over the whole table and dumping a jug of forget-me-nots right in the middle of it. Then she set two long-stemmed glasses beside the cutlery, pouring apple juice for Ellen and wine for herself.

As they ate, Ellen started telling her mother about a playful kitten one of the Proctor twins had brought into school. 'I think we should have a kitten, Mummy,' she said. 'Only I don't want a dozy old tea-cosy one like Granny Carson's. Maybe we should hold auditions or something to make sure we got a really funny one, like Jenny's.'

Tickled at the thought, Cass choked and laughed out loud, then caught herself, her hand to her mouth, as Ellen stared back at her in astonishment.

'Oh, Ellen,' Cass cried then, remorsefully, 'what an

awful time you've had and I haven't been able to help you at all, have I? Not at all. We've been like a pair of lost, lonely ghosts.'

Next day Ellen came home to find Cass in the act of cutting her wheat-coloured hair level with her ears, already panicking at her own impulsiveness.

'I don't know why, I just had to. I couldn't wait. What d'you think?' asked Cass. 'Have I missed any?'

'Just here,' said Ellen. 'Right at the back. A long, long wispy bit. Stay still – I'll do it.' She snipped gently and exactly.

'Is it OK now?' Cass peered at herself in the mirror, fluffing her hair up from the crown to make it wavy.

'Yes. I like it. Honestly. Only I've never seen you with short hair before. You look really different. Nice but different. There's more of your face.'

They both giggled nervously.

'I know, to celebrate my haircut we'll have supper at The Eel's Foot, like we used to, do you remember, Nell?' said Cass. 'I wonder if that barman still makes his diabolical-looking purple drink for children?'

'Oh, Mum, really, Purple Passion,' said Ellen pulling a face. 'It was only blackcurrant and lemonade, you know. He just invented it to make little kids feel important. Hey, do you realise you got the name of the pub right, that time, Mum? You always called it The Eel in the Boot before!'

'Well, that's because of the stupid pub sign,' said Cass defensively. 'It's what it looks like. It really is confusing. Yes it *is*! Don't you dare laugh at me, you horrible superior child . . .'

The day after, when Ellen returned from school, she found a row of bulging dustbin bags neatly stacked beside the bins.

'Old clothes,' said Cass, finding her daughter staring. 'I'm just not that dressy kind of person any more. I know I should send them to Oxfam but I couldn't stand them in the house for another single minute. And, Ellen,' she called super-casually as Ellen went into the house, heading for the stairs. 'I've – er – cleared out Lily's room.'

But Cass had done more than that.

The nest bed was gone, the curtains taken down and in Ellen's absence the walls had been painted a simple buttery white.

And however hard Ellen stared at them she could find no trace of silvery boughs, ferns, or rushy pools. Just an empty, sunlit room, its plain walls glistening faintly with still-wet emulsion.

It's not haunted any more, she thought. It's just a room. A normal, empty room. And though this should have been a relief, all she felt was the dull ache of losing Lily forever.

Cass came up behind Ellen and, bending, put her arms right round her, gently leaning her chin on her daughter's shoulder.

'I thought it was time,' she said quietly. 'It was so hard for me to let those dreams go, Nell. But they were just my dreams, you see. Not Tom's. This house was what I dreamed of for us all and I wanted that dream so much I didn't let myself see – oh, far too many things. And to make my dreams come true your dad had to – oh, he – ' Cass stopped, took a deep breath and repeated, 'I thought it was time. When we move house next time, Nell, we'll make it beautiful, I promise. But not – not like Midsummer House. And now that I've discovered I'm really a gardener I'm determined to have a lovely garden too. Even if it's a tiny one.'

But Ellen was thinking quickly. 'Move house – do you mean a house without Daddy? Is that what you mean?'

'Maybe,' said Cass, biting her lip briefly. 'Maybe. Yes. That would probably be best.'

'Oh,' said Ellen, too politely, 'I see.'

'I thought you would have guessed,' said Cass, moving away restlessly, wrapping her arms around her own body now. 'I thought it would be obvious.'

'Not really,' said Ellen. 'No it wasn't. I didn't think. I didn't think about it really.'

She felt as if she was flashing past herself on a train; dark light, dark light. Everything was happening too fast. She couldn't take it in. She wanted to press herself against the walls of Lily's room. She needed something solid to lean on. She wanted to crawl into bed in the dark and never have to think or feel again.

'I met someone who might be interested in buying the house, actually,' said Cass. 'They'd like to use it for city children. A sort of centre for them to learn about the countryside. Wouldn't that be nice?'

'Yes,' said Ellen, closing her eyes to stop the flashing-train feeling. 'Yes yes yes.'

It was nearly midsummer. The weather was perfect. Cass worked out in the garden almost all day now until the light was gone. She was no longer the haggard, sleepwalking woman she had been after Lily's disappearance. But nor was Cass the light-hearted, impulsive person she had seemed to be before they moved to Midsummer House. Her solitary hours out of doors with the sun, wind and open air were changing her into someone else entirely. And that new someone was a total mystery to Ellen.

Ellen didn't ask her mother why, if they were

planning to move away soon, she was taking so much trouble with the garden. But one day she overheard Cass talking to herself as she dug and weeded amongst the old-fashioned roses. 'Nell was right,' she said aloud. 'There were far too many water plants. Why did I do that? And why lilies when I could have chosen jasmine or roses? I wish I'd chosen roses. I should have filled her room with them.'

And Ellen realised Cass had not forgotten Lily, nor even wanted to. She was just trying to find a way to go on living without her. Trying to find new, more realistic dreams than the old ones. And the garden was helping her get well keeping her busy until she knew what those dreams might be.

One morning Ellen woke to find sunlight lying across her face and hands. Screwing up her eyes against the dazzle even before she opened them, she found herself smiling as if, in her dreams, she had been talking to someone she loved.

'It's Midsummer's Eve,' she whispered, remembering, her skin prickling.

And she knew she had to get up now and go out into the garden where someone or something was waiting for her. There was no whispering voice or ghostly shadow this time, just the urgent knowledge that there was something important for her to do and no time to lose.

Outdoors the garden glinted with dew, every leaf and blade of grass a brilliant mirror. Birds called to one another, rapid, fluid notes. Under the trees a blue haze gathered in pools. As always she felt the bluebells before she saw them, their colour streaming into her like a cool scent; their fragrance, even as they faded in the dry midsummer weather, a sweet, wordless language. Everything in the garden was calling out to her, she thought, in its own way. The ancient trees, crawling beetles, the flushed petals of the daisies. Under her feet the grass felt springy, cushioned.

For just a moment, alone in the early-morning garden, Ellen caught a glimpse of how Lily might feel, safely dwelling among swans. For this one moment Ellen too could believe not just that the earth was alive in every blade of grass but that it was holding her up, supporting her, even caring for her. She realised then that she had never really known her little sister, as she had also never truly known Cass. But she loved them both as she still loved her troubled, far-away father. They were her family. All the family she would ever have.

Follow the signs.

Follow the signs.

Across the sparkling garden something caught the corner of her eye. Its blue was not the deeper blue of the bluebells, but misty and faded like speedwell. It fluttered out of the apple trees, alighting on a William Lobb moss rose Cass had been weeding round the evening before, where it seemed to wait to be noticed.

Follow the signs.

'A blue butterfly,' Ellen whispered, remembering the butterfly beating against the window the day Lily vanished. It had been too soon then, but now –

The butterfly opened and closed its wings briefly, then it was off again in such expressive circles, Ellen imagined it leaving a coloured ribbon-like trail in the air.

It wants me to follow, she realised incredulously. No sooner had she completed the thought than it stopped circling and headed purposefully away from the roses.

'I'm coming. I'm coming,' she said breathlessly.

Zipping across the lawn, her butterfly seemed to be leading her out of the garden entirely, into the deep green lane. Momentarily she lost it, then caught sight of it pulsing gently on a branch of elderflower.

As soon as she caught up, it fluttered high above the lane, out of her reach, careering ahead on a wild, zigzag course. Ellen was giggling by this time, half believing in this strange new game she was playing, half convinced she was crazy. But whenever she slowed down, deciding she had had enough, the butterfly danced around her head in apparent impatience until she showed signs of following again. She chased after her butterfly messenger for almost a mile in this way.

Suddenly it veered off into the trees and without a moment's hesitation Ellen plunged after it.

The earth was soft and damp. Shallow streams criss-crossed the marshy ground. The sound of trickling water filled the air. Light dappled her arms. The air was sharp with pine and leaf mould. In the dim light under thickly-growing oaks and larches, the butterfly flickered in and out of sight ahead of her, scarcely more visible than a moth.

In places the little wood was so dark, wild roses shone like stars against their unkempt bushes. A towering pillar of a holly tree had been transformed into a ghostly waterfall by honeysuckle twining down through its branches. Once she saw fox cubs in a clearing, their fur bracken-coloured in the filtered sunlight. As Ellen passed in pursuit of her butterfly, they gazed after her with golden eyes, one cub still thoughtfully chewing on its brother's tail. Once she drew in her breath sharply as an adder glided in front of her feet. Later still a heron slowly flapped along at her side until it found some business of its own in a dank-looking pool.

'They're not afraid of me,' she thought, amazed. 'Nothing in this wood is even a little bit afraid of me.'

It was like being allowed to glimpse the garden of the world before human history began. If a bird or hare spoke to her now, Ellen was sure that she, like Misha, would understand its speech.

We're going to Marsh Mary's, she thought suddenly. But by a back way. A secret way.

Then, as the trees thinned and the salt tang reached her on the quickening wind, her butterfly took off erratically, joyously, over her head, skimmed a clump of foxgloves and vanished into the trees.

And Ellen was on her own again.

Is it some kind of illness I've got, Ellen wondered drearily, as she picked her way through drifts of stitchwort and clambered over a fallen tree to where the gorse bushes began. Is it an illness that makes me keep on hoping, even when there's nothing to hope for?

Head down in her despair, slithering down the sandy, heathery slope increasingly out of control, Ellen failed to see the person standing beside the upturned boats at the back of Marsh Mary's shack until he put out his hand to steady her.

'Well, you look just like Ellen,' he said. 'And you are one of the three people in the world I most wanted to see. But it can't really be you, can it? So I'm probably dreaming that I'm here in Suffolk, after all.'

But Ellen had to stare for some moments before she could speak. And even then there were no words to say what was in her heart. So she simply threw her arms around her father's neck and hugged him until she could be absolutely sure that he was real.

11

The Shining Ones

'I couldn't sleep,' he said. 'I suddenly had this strong feeling I had to be here with you and Cass, and all the sensible reasons I've been giving myself for staying in London these last months didn't seem nearly so sensible any more. So I just got in the car and came right down here to the shore. I've been here quite a while. I watched the sun come up.'

'Why didn't you come home,' said Ellen, 'if you wanted to be with us?'

He shook his head. 'I couldn't when it came to it. I didn't know how, after – after everything. Do you know, I always forget how huge the sky seems here. And the air ... Anyway – for pete's sake, Ellen, what are you doing wandering around the countryside on your own at this time of the morning?'

But Ellen didn't answer him. 'It's Midsummer's Eve,' she said urgently. 'I've got the feeling Marsh Mary's expecting us. She's got a boat, you see. I think she'll let us use it. It's all right, Daddy, I can row if you don't know how.'

And without any further explanation she led her bemused father to the shabby upside-down ark of a house where Marsh Mary was waiting, her face expressionless, her arms folded across her chest.

Marsh Mary didn't bother with introductions. She stared at Ellen's father with eyes as unblinking as Boris the seagull's and demanded, indicating Ellen, 'Did she fetch you down here or did you come of your own choosing?'

And as if this cantankerous marsh witch had a right to interrogate him, Tom Carson replied quietly, 'No, I somehow had to come. For some reason I can't understand, I simply knew I had to be here. I've been driving half the night.'

'Then there might be some small glimmer of hope for you,' Mary muttered grimly, half to herself. 'Ellen, you can take my boat. I'll be waiting for you when you get back.'

'I'm not even going to ask where you're taking me,' her father said as between them they eased the dinghy away from the shore. 'Because I still feel as though this might turn out to be a dream and I know that if I ask too many questions I'll only wake up.'

The water was green, silky, shot through with brilliant splinters of sunlight. Further out a purling mist still clung to the reeds, gently enclosing Ellen and her father in a private watery world.

No birds sang. But they were watching, Ellen thought. Watching, listening from their rushy haunts.

'It's not a dream, Daddy,' said Ellen. 'It's true. And we're going to the island where the swans are keeping Lily.'

Her father closed his eyes. 'Oh, so it is a dream, after all,' he said to himself. 'A strange, beautiful dream. And in a minute I'll wake up to the sound of the phone ringing or someone hammering on my door to ask me questions from some newspaper. But I don't want to wake. Not yet.'

If her father was so convinced this was a dream, Ellen thought, perhaps this was a safe time to say some of the things she'd kept locked inside herself these last months.

'It's all been lopsided at our house, Daddy, you know,' she said urgently. 'It's always been Cass. What she thinks she wants. What she dreams. Like living in a world where there's only one time of day. Where the moon shines brighter than the sun. And you *pretended* it was what you wanted, too. You never once said it wasn't, did you? And the worse things got, the more you worked and worked and shut yourself away and never once told us what *you* wanted, what you dreamed.'

'Ellen, that's because –' he said painfully, looking away from her, ' – that's because I didn't know myself, sweetheart. I don't think I've ever known. At least not since I was about your age. Somehow, without ever meaning to, I turned into this desperate person who only knew how to work and earn money. Of the two of us Cass always seemed the one who really knew how to live. And I suppose, when I met her, I sort of hoped she could do it for both of us. I didn't even want to have to think about what kind of work I was doing, you see. That's how I came to do – what I did. It was just a building to me, then. Only another kind of building. And then it went all wrong. Some things can't ever truly be put right, Ellen. Like those terrible oil slicks spreading across the sea for miles, trapping birds and seals, poisoning everything in their path. I made myself a small part of something that has done – is still doing – a great deal of harm. But what can I do? It's too late.'

He sounds like Marsh Mary, Ellen thought, telling me all the words have been spoken and all the stories told. And he believed what he was saying, she could see.

'We needed you, you know,' Ellen said quietly. 'Me and Lily and Cass. We always needed you. It was all *wrong* without you. Mum's lovely but when the three of us had to try to be a family without you – it was –' She searched for words to describe the way it had felt. It was, she thought, as if Midsummer House, like the castle in a fairy tale, had fallen under an enchantment, a wistful, anxious half-sleep, where no one could ever be who he or she truly was.

' – like rowing with one oar,' said Tom Carson unexpectedly before she could speak her thoughts out loud. 'That's what it felt like to me, living without you all. It took so much unbelievably hard work just to keep going round and round in the same old circle. I'm sorry, Ellen. I'm so sorry, sweetheart. I can't begin to tell you how much I wish I could turn the clock back and do things differently.'

'I know,' said Ellen painfully. 'I know you're really sorry now.'

Supposing I can't do this after all, she thought in terror. Supposing it's like last time and it all goes wrong and I just make everything worse. I wish Misha was here.

But aloud she said only, 'I think we'd better be quiet now, Daddy. I think we're supposed to listen.'

Her father looked curiously peaceful, she thought. Despite his long night drive, he looked less tired than he had done for years.

They rested their oars, letting the slow current take them.

Someone's cleared away the waterweed, and that awful junk, Ellen thought with surprise. The stream was flowing so freely now, the water so clear, that amongst the dark meshes of the reeds, the vast sky seemed to float beneath the boat as well as above it.

Then the thought came to her.

The water's alive! It's alive – and it knows us. Who we are and why we're here. 'Daddy,' she whispered urgently. 'Do you ever think everything's alive? Not just people. But places. Can places feel, can they *talk*?'

'Some people believe everything has a spirit,' he whispered back. 'In India they call them devas, the Shining Ones. They're a kind of guardian, of trees, rivers, gardens, even houses.'

'But do *you* believe it?' Ellen insisted. Remembering the fleeting magical being who had haunted Midsummer House before it was tamed, she badly needed to know. 'Could those spirits talk to us? Could they try to make humans listen to them? Try to get us to change?'

And could those invisible Shining Ones make a sad, mixed-up family move all the way down to Suffolk to put something right that had gone badly wrong long, long ago, she thought. Could they wait patiently for years and years until a funny, special little girl was born to that family? A star child who somehow never forgot, like most other people forget, that she belonged to the wild and human, the visible and invisible worlds. A child who understood the language of swans.

Her father looked around him at the marsh steeped in its green midsummer silence. As she waited for his reply, Ellen felt the quickening rhythm of her heart. Tell the truth, she prayed. Please, please tell the truth. Because I think Lily's with the Shining Ones now, and they're listening and she'll know, she always knows, when anybody lies.

At last Tom Carson gave a wary smile. 'Why have I got this terrifying feeling that I must answer all those questions absolutely truthfully?' he said awkwardly.

'As if this is some kind of ancient and dangerous riddle and I'll wind up dangling by my ankles from a tall tree if I fail.'

He passed his hand unhappily through his hair.

A dragonfly hovered in the air, only inches ahead of the slowly moving boat. Are you another messenger, Ellen wondered. Like my butterfly? Is everything in the world either a message or a messenger, if we could only be bothered to understand it?

The silence of the marsh was deepening with every passing moment. It's listening, she thought. They are listening, the Shining Ones. Listening to our thoughts. We don't have to speak even a single word, they know us so well.

She recognised where they were now, but still allowed the water to take them where it would, waiting, dry mouthed, for her father's answer.

'Do you mean do I believe it when I'm here?' he said finally. 'Here, now, with you? Or do you mean back in London with the phone ringing and all the gutter press after my blood?'

Ellen looked away to hide her grin. That was her dad all over. Always insisting on precise information.

'Both,' she said at once, mercilessly. 'Here *and* there.'

The boat was moving surprisingly swiftly now. The current must be stronger than she thought. It was strange she had never noticed it before. There seemed no need to touch the oars at all.

'Here, at this moment with you,' Tom Carson said, finally, 'in this green, magical place, I believe absolutely that everything is living and that every living thing has a spirit. It's so simple and right. Like coming home. Like the dreams I had as a child where I could fly or – or understand the speech of animals. But

118

when I go back to London – ' he shook his head. 'Honestly, Ellen. If I believed it there, how could I possibly go on living the way I do? I'd either go mad or I'd have to – I'd have to change completely . . .' His voice faded away, puzzled, as if he was listening to the words he had released into the air, finding something in them he had not expected.

The boat went on floating freely downstream, travelling faster still, and with renewed determination, Ellen thought, as if magically guided by those invisible spirits of wind and water.

He told the truth after all and now they're taking us, she told herself dreamily. The Shining Ones are taking us to the island of the wild swans.

But I didn't bring anything to get through the brambles, Ellen realised, with a guilty jolt. I didn't know I was going to need it.

And she was going to ask her father, without any real hope now, if he had a pocketknife with him, anything at all that might help them hack their way through the impenetrable briars, only somehow she had left it too late. With the inevitability that so often comes in bad dreams, and with the same nightmare speed, the boat was already rushing headlong into the impossibly narrow channel between the swan island and its neighbour.

We've got to stop, thought Ellen. We're going to be cut to pieces!

But the cruel barrier was already looming over them, the hooked thorns like claws that would wound and tear. With a small scream Ellen ducked down, pulling her father with her, covering her head with her arms in a vain effort to protect herself.

The agonising collision never came.

Instead the boat travelled smoothly on through

briars that parted gently like a secret gateway, on and on towards the hidden inlet of the swans' island, where it came to rest.

And there, making her way gravely towards them, amongst wings that lifted like waves to let her pass, and long necks that arched gracefully to allow her safely through, was Lily.

She was taller now, her hair slightly darker, her skin lightly golden from the sun. And whether or not it was true, afterwards, whenever Ellen pictured that reunion she always mysteriously saw her little sister with wild flowers and leaves fastened into her uncombed hair.

But there were no feathers, no pinions. Lily had not, after all, as Ellen had secretly feared, grown wings to keep her in the swans' wild world forever. Her small sister was simply and completely human; both her dirty narrow feet planted firmly on the ground.

And her eyes shone with humour and determination as she said very clearly, 'Daddy. Ellen. Home.'

Waiting on Mary's front step, tousling the ears of her latest pup, Misha saw them climbing the steep sandy path between the gorse bushes.

'They're coming. She's with them,' he called excitedly into the house. 'He's carrying her on his shoulders. She's sticking her hands right over his eyes and he's laughing his head off. Ellen's doing a crazy dance all around them. Her face looks quite different when she laughs. Like another person. Mary, do you think they'll be OK? Will they stay at Midsummer House after all? Will he change? Do you really think he will?'

Catching his mood the puppy began jumping up at him, trying to lick his face, barking comically in its tiny yipping voice.

'For heaven's sake, how can a person write even a single intelligent sentence, with this racket going on?' said Mary, emerging querulously.

But she too gazed thoughtfully after Ellen, Lily and Tom Carson as they carried on past her house at a little distance, without stopping, and after a moment she said matter of factly, 'Maybe. Who knows? Anything's possible. If I've learned anything at all, Misha, it's that we are always part of a far bigger story than we know.'

Watching his friend dance out of sight, wondering a little sadly if she'd even noticed him waiting for her, Misha suddenly heard what Mary had said.

'Writing?' he said, grinning all over his face. 'Mary, did I hear you say *writing*?'

'Daddy,' said Ellen urgently, as they reached the path that led back to where her father had parked the car. 'Would you mind very much if I went back to Mary's house for a little while. I need to talk to a friend. Would that be OK?'

Her father shook his head. 'I'm going to leave the car where it is for now,' he said. 'I'm not ready to put this precious small person down just yet. What I'm going to do is amble slowly along the lanes with my younger daughter here, and we're going to pick your mother a great big bunch of every kind of wild flower we can find and I'm going to see if I can just keep on dreaming this amazing beautiful dream for as long as I possibly can. So don't worry about us, you just come along whenever you're ready.'

'I keep telling you, Tom Carson,' said Ellen laughing. 'But you won't listen. You *aren't* dreaming!'

Just before she was out of earshot she remembered something else and yelled at the top of her voice, dancing backwards down the slope, 'Daddy – you'd better go round the back when you get there. Mum's out in the garden most days. And I'm warning you, she'll be wearing the most disgusting, shabbiest old jeans you ever saw in your *life!*'

Then she started running, towards the sandy margin between the marshes and the sea, where smoke rose from a corrugated tin roof and both her friends were waiting.